"Am I Forgiven?" Brace Asked With A Grin.

"Forgiven?" Frances repeated. "Oh, for being a jerk, you mean?" She smiled. "Well…I don't suppose you can help it. But I wish you'd make up your mind whether I'm friend or foe, because it gets a little tiresome trying to figure out whether to feed you or run for cover."

"You're offering me a choice? Then I say we settle for friends."

But don't count on it, lady, Brace thought. Whatever it was he wanted from her, he was pretty sure it wasn't friendship. But it would do—until he could figure out what it was about this one ordinary woman that had burrowed under his skin until he couldn't get her off his mind, asleep or awake….

Dear Reader,

This month it seems like everyone's in romantic trouble. We have runaway brides and jilted grooms....They've been left at the altar and wonder if they'll *ever* find true love with the right person.

Of course they do, and we get to find out how, as we read Silhouette Desire's delightful month of "Jilted!" heroes and heroines.

And what better way to start this special month than with *The Accidental Bridegroom*, a second 1994 *Man of the Month* from one of your favorites, Ann Major? I'm sure you'll enjoy this passionate story of seduction and supposed betrayal as much as I do.

And look for five more fabulous books by some of your most beloved writers: Dixie Browning, Cait London, Raye Morgan, Jennifer Greene and Cathie Linz. Yes, their characters might have been left at the altar...but they don't stay single for long!

So don't pick and choose—read about them all! I loved these stories, and I'm sure you will, too.

Lucia Macro
Senior Editor

Please address questions and book requests to:
Silhouette Reader Service
U.S.: 3010 Walden Ave., P.O. Box 1325, Buffalo, NY 14269
Canadian: P.O. Box 609, Fort Erie, Ont. L2A 5X3

DIXIE BROWNING
TWO HEARTS, SLIGHTLY USED

SILHOUETTE *Desire*

Published by Silhouette Books
America's Publisher of Contemporary Romance

SILHOUETTE BOOKS

ISBN 0-373-05890-X

TWO HEARTS, SLIGHTLY USED

Copyright © 1994 by Dixie Browning

DIXIE BROWNING

has written over fifty books for Silhouette since 1980. She is a charter member of the Romance Writers of America and an award-winning author who has toured extensively for Silhouette Books. She also writes historical romances with her sister, under the name Bronwyn Williams.

One

It might as well be the end of the world. There wasn't a ferry slip, much less a bridge. Frances Smith Jones, surrounded by the bulk of her worldly possessions, stood at the edge of the weathered pier and stared across at the dusky smudge on the horizon that was Coronoke Island, waiting for the boy from the marina to bring around a boat.

Only a few days ago, burning her bridges behind her had seemed like a terrific idea. Now she was beginning to wonder if she hadn't made one more king-size mistake.

Massaging the pucker between her eyebrows, she pushed back the headache that had been threatening all day, then discreetly rubbed her sore bottom. One thing was certain: if she had to start over again—and she did—it would most definitely *not* be as a long-haul truck driver!

"I can tote part of that stuff over for you, ma'am, but you'll have to leave the rest here. All I got in the water right now is the thirteen-footer, and she don't have a lot of freeboard. Choppy as it is today, we'd take on too much water."

His name was Jerry. She had caught him just as he was locking the tiny marina office for the day and asked him where the bridge to Coronoke was located. "Bridge to Coronoke? Ma'am, that thing washed out back when I was in sixth grade. There was talk of re-building it for a while, but the state wouldn't spend the money, and the cottagers over there sorta liked the privacy. I can run you over, but you'll have to wait till tomorrow evening for the rest of your stuff, unless you want to take one of Maudie's boats and haul 'em yourself. I got a date tonight and school tomorrow." He grinned self-consciously, big white teeth gleaming in a perennially tanned face.

Frances put his age at about seventeen, though he looked younger. She herself was thirty-nine, and at the moment she felt every single minute of it.

Indicating her smallest suitcase, the groceries she'd bought in the village and her laptop computer—things she could not do without—she locked the rest in the trunk of her car. She could get through the night on the bare essentials and worry about the rest tomorrow.

Dusk was falling rapidly, thanks in part to the heavy layer of clouds that had moved in late in the after-noon. She hadn't counted on having to find her un-cle's cottage in the dark. According to him, there were five cottages and a sort of lodge on the island. No street numbers, no street lights, no streets.

"Ask Maudie," he had told her. "You'll find her at the Hunt."

Well, first she had to *find* Maudie, and to do that she had to find something called a hunt. Or was it a hut? Probably the lodge he'd mentioned.

It had all seemed so simple when she'd handed in her resignation, met with the lawyer to sign over the house to the Joneses, called Uncle Seymore in Philadelphia to ask if he still had that cottage somewhere down South and, if so, was it rented and, if not, could she please possibly borrow it for a few weeks, just until she decided what she was going to do with the rest of her life?

She had offered to pay rent and utilities, although it would've eaten into her cash reserve, but Uncle Seymore wouldn't hear of it. "Bake me something tasty for Christmas," he'd said, and she had promised, without the least notion of where she would be in a year's time. High on a heady mixture of optimism, outrage and blind determination, she had managed to convince herself that, free at last, she was embarking on the adventure of a lifetime.

But somewhere between Fort Wayne, Indiana, and Coronoke, North Carolina—after two flat tires, numerous wrong turns, half a bottle of aspirin and a near miss from a driver who evidently suffered under the misassumption that the entire Indiana highway system constituted the Indianapolis Speedway—her taste for adventure had begun to dissipate.

And then she'd had to pick up that small-town weekly paper in a fast-food restaurant in Manteo, with the picture of a buck-toothed, hair-ribboned child and the too-cute headline of Lordy, Lordy, Look Who's Forty!

Who needed reminding?

Clutching her precious laptop computer as they roared across the rough expanse of open water, Frances wondered at what point her brain had begun to atrophy. The eldest of five, she'd always been considered the sensible member of the rowdy Smith brood. Sweet, docile Frances, practical to the core.

For docile, read doormat!

Apprehension grew as they neared the small, wooded island. The only sign of habitation was the pier, and that was deserted. Club Med, this was not!

She settled up the tab, hoping she wouldn't need to call on Jerry's services too often. "Where will I find someone named Maudie?" she asked, once she and her belongings had been set off onto the narrow pier. She was shivering with cold, her hair was dripping with salt spray and her poor derriere had been pounded flat on the unpadded aluminum seat.

"Utah. Gone to see her new granddaughter."

"Utah! Oh, marvelous. Then perhaps you can tell me where to find the Seymore cottage. I think it's called Blackbeard's Retreat, or something like that."

"Hole. Old Teach weren't one to do much retreatin', not even when Lieutenant Meynard come at him with a head-remover. Whole thing happened just a little ways down the sound, right abreast—"

Frances was in no mood for a blow-by-blow of some dead pirate's Waterloo. "Well, whatever it's called, where do I find it?"

"Sorry, ma'am. Some folks likes hearing about that kind of stuff, some don't. You take that there path through the woods—" he pointed at an all-but-invisible thinning of the dense, shadowy forest "—and then hang a right. Cottages are all on the other side of the island. Blackbeard's Hole's the one on the end. Green striped storm blinds. Can't miss it." Mission accomplished, he jumped back into the boat and prepared to cast off.

Standing forlornly on the pier, surrounded by her assorted belongings, Frances was sorely tempted to toss it all into the boat and go back with him. She could spend the night at a motel on Hatteras. Things were bound to look better in the morning. They could hardly look worse.

"Jerry, do you think—" she began, just as he opened the throttle and flipped her a jaunty salute.

"See you later, ma'am! Gotta go pick up my date!"

"Oh, for pity's sake! If that's Southern hospitality, they can just—just *stuff* it!" she muttered as the roar of the outboard diminished in the distance.

The first indication that she was not alone came when she felt the vibration of heavy footsteps on the sturdy wooden pier.

"If you're looking for the Keegans, they're not here. If you're looking for a motel, we don't have any. If you're looking for hospitality, Southern or otherwise, we're fresh out of that, too. Sorry, lady. You got off at the wrong stop."

Her first impression was of a tall man who could easily have carried another fifteen or twenty pounds on his rangy frame. A nondescript sweatshirt hung from a set of wide, square shoulders. Worn jeans loosely covered lean hips and long legs. His boots, the thick-soled, step-in variety, showed signs of long, hard wear. Even without the extra weight he needed, he was a big man, towering over her own five foot eight, which had recently gone from slender to downright skinny.

A matched pair of Jack Spratts, she thought, with a wild urge to giggle. Frances had never giggled in her life. At least, not since she'd left the third grade. "The Keegans? Would that, by any chance, include a Maudie?"

He was closer now. The light was at his back, but what she could see of his expression was definitely not encouraging. Ignoring her perfectly civil question, he said, "I told you, lady, this place is battened down for the winter. No phones, no power, no people. You want to try again after Memorial Day, you might get a better reception."

It could hardly be worse. The thought echoed again in her aching head. The raw wind that had followed her all the way down the narrow strip of barrier islands had diminished somewhat with the setting of the sun, but the cold had long since penetrated her layers of spray-damp clothing. Her nose had probably turned blue to match the circles under her eyes. Nothing like making a good first impression.

"And how do you propose I leave?" she inquired sweetly. To anyone who knew her, such a reckless disregard for danger would be a sure tip-off of how near the end of her rope she was. "Perhaps you'd be so kind as to direct me to the nearest bus stop?"

He didn't know her, and obviously didn't care to. His response was brief, rude and unhelpful. In the rapidly fading light, Frances couldn't tell much about his face, except that it reminded her of the chunk of petrified wood her grandmother used to use as a doorstop.

"Sorry to disappoint you, but I have no intention of doing any such thing," she said, her attempt at firmness largely ruined by the chattering of her teeth. "If you'll just point me in the right direction, I'll find the place, myself."

When he continued to stand there, arms crossed over his broad chest, she said, "It's the Seymore cottage. It's called Blackbeard's Hole. It's the one with the green-striped shutters!"

Exasperated beyond bearing, she reached down and began gathering up her assorted baggage. "Oh, forget it! I'll just—"

"Storm blinds."

"What? Oh, never mind, I'll find it myself!" she snapped. Her head ached, she was cold, hungry, discouraged and bone tired after two and a half days of traveling. It had been a real bitch of a week.

A real bitch of a decade, actually, but she had made up her mind to leave the past behind her and look ahead to the next forty years. They were going to be terrific! She owed herself that much.

Gathering up her computer and her suitcase, Frances eyed the lumpy sacks of groceries, glanced at the sky and prayed for the rain to hold off until she had everything under cover. Her unwelcoming committee obviously had no intention of helping her.

So be it. Brushing past him, she set out up the sloping beach toward the narrow path Jerry had pointed out. If the cottages were on the other side of the island, why the dickens hadn't he driven his blooming boat around there and parked it closer to her doorstep?

The owners liked their privacy, he'd said. Well, if she had any choice in the matter, they could keep their darned privacy! Not even a decent sidewalk! Her shoes were filled with sand before she'd gone a hundred feet, and there was no telling how much farther she still had to go.

"You really intend to go through with it, huh?"

At the sound of that gravelly voice right behind her, Frances almost walked into a tree. And that was another thing about sand she hated! A body could sneak up on you and you wouldn't even hear him!

Trudging onward, she made up her mind to ignore him, but the temptation was too great. She stole a glance over her shoulder and then had the grace to feel ashamed when she saw that he was carrying the two largest of her six sacks of groceries. They were heavy, too. Five pounds of this, five pounds of that, not to mention all the canned goods—she'd had to start from scratch and stock up on everything.

He moved up beside her, crowding her between the dark, encroaching bushes. "How do you intend to get in?" he asked.

Frances tried to ignore the feeling of being trapped in the forest with a hungry predator. She refused to be intimidated. She'd come too far for that. "I'll pick the lock, of course. Or if I can't find my trusty lock picker, I'll just toss a brick through a window." A streak of reckless perversity that was totally out of character kept her from mentioning the key her uncle had mailed her.

"That's what storm blinds are for."

"Oh? Then it'll have to be lock-picking. I always hate picking strange locks in the dark, but at least it's neater than using explosives."

Explosives? The closest she'd ever come to using explosives was when she'd microwaved her first egg. She was running on adrenaline, practically begging for trouble from a stranger who looked as if he'd invented trouble and still held the patent.

But anger served to keep her going, and she was afraid if she slowed down for so much as a minute, she might collapse like a punctured balloon.

"Look, I have a key from the owner, all right?" she cried, exasperated. "I'm not trespassing, so you can just knock off the watchdog routine!"

He shrugged. "Maybe. Maybe not. Might as well warn you, though, if you're looking for a cozy place to crash—the generator tank probably needs filling, and without that, you won't have lights, heat or running water. You might find a candle or two, but that's about all."

"Fine! Just give me the luxuries of life, and I'll do without the necessities." The only luxury she wanted at the moment was a bed and a roof over her head, and even the roof was optional as long as it didn't rain. "I'll figure it all out tomorrow." Fumbling in her shoulder bag, she came up with the door key and prayed it was the right one. Knowing Uncle Seymore, it could just as easily be the key to his own basement. Poor Uncle Seymore wasn't quite as sharp as he used to be.

It was the right key. Frances stepped inside and drew a deep breath of relief. Home at long last! And then she shivered. Home, at the moment, was cold as a tomb, damp as a well and smelled of mice and mildew. "I've seen cozier caves," she muttered. "Do bats smell like mice?"

"I warned you." He had come in right behind her, and for one crazy moment, she was glad of his nearness. Alone wasn't quite so intimidating when there was someone there to share it.

"So you did. Did I remember to thank you? No? Then thank you so much for all your help and your warm welcome. Now, if you don't mind, I'd like to get the rest of my groceries under cover in case it rains tonight."

"I think that's pretty well guaranteed. Do you have a flashlight?"

"Of course I have a flashlight!" Digging in her purse, she came up with a small plastic model designed to locate car keys and keyholes. It illuminated a spot roughly the size of a nickel.

"Pretty. By the way, does your keeper know you've escaped?"

Frances could have wept—not so much at her own stupidity, but because he was there to gloat over it. Her good flashlight was back in Fort Wayne, along with her books, her mother's good chesterfield, Aunt Becky's marble-topped table, her AM-FM radio and all her garden implements. She'd been so blessed eager to escape with a clear conscience that she'd given her in-laws practically everything that could even faintly be considered marital property and stored the rest.

"Oh, yes. I left word at the asylum I'd be leaving. So thanks again for all your kind assistance," she said with a saccharine smile. It was almost too dark to see inside the house, even with the front door standing wide open. She flicked on a light switch. Nothing happened.

"I warned you." He was still holding both sacks of groceries, and she caught the gleam of a smile—a malicious smile, she told herself.

"Lucky for me, I'm not afraid of the dark." She was afraid of three things—snakes, lightning and being made a fool of again. "Just put them anywhere—on that counter over there."

"I may as well go get—"

"No, thank you. I need the exercise." She held the door wide, hoping her grimace would pass for a smile in the dim light. In about five seconds she was going to cry, curse or kick something—*hard!* And she'd just as soon not have any witnesses.

Back at the Hunt several minutes later, Brace let himself inside and reached automatically for the light switch. His hand fell to his side, closed into a fist and then slid into his pocket. Dammit, his conscience was already giving him flak for all the lies he'd laid on her, and the crazy thing was, he didn't even possess a conscience!

If she was still here tomorrow, he promised himself he would check out her generator. The tank wasn't empty. They were kept topped off to prevent condensation.

Of course, he could simply flip the breakers and she wouldn't need a generator. Unless the power cut out. Keegan had explained how salt buildup could cause transformers to arc, setting off pole fires, but there'd been enough rain lately to wash the salt off the lines.

On the other hand, there was no point in making things too easy for her. The more uncomfortable she was, the sooner she'd head back to wherever she'd come from. If there was one thing Brace didn't need right now, it was company! Keegan had sworn the place was deserted by all but a few die-hard hunters in the wintertime.

Using his excellent night vision, he made his way to the back part of the restored central section of the lodge called Keegan's Hunt. It had been built about a hundred years ago as a private hunting club and was on the way to falling into ruins when Rich Keegan, a few generations removed from the original builder, had come down to see if there was anything worth salvaging before the family's ninety-nine-year lease ran out.

He'd found a squatter named Maudie—a divorcee with a grown daughter—married her and begun the task of rebuilding the elegant old hunt club and establishing a small but thriving air-commuter service between Billy Mitchell Airport on Hatteras and the mainland.

Not until Brace reached his own room, a corridor-like affair with a single oddly placed window, did he switch on a light, confident that it wouldn't be seen from cottage row. Standing before a bow-fronted, bird's-eye maple bureau with an ornate, gilt-framed mirror above it, he studied his own face dispassionately for the first time since he'd arrived a week and a half ago to island-sit for the Keegans while they went West.

It had been pretty dark. He figured she couldn't have gotten a good look at him. Too bad. Stroking his jaw, he told himself that if she'd come a little earlier in the day, he could've scared the hell out of her without having to lay on all those lies. The way Brace figured it, in the long run the truth was a lot easier than lies. He'd never been a candidate for sainthood, but at least he drew the line somewhere.

Dispassionately he studied the image in the clouded and speckled old mirror. A few parts of the face that stared back were familiar. The deep-set gray eyes, narrowed from years of squinting against the sun. The hairline that was just beginning to migrate northward—at least, he imagined it was. As for the hair itself, it was still thick, of a nondescript shade of brown that turned paler on top in the summer sun. The gray hardly showed, not that he gave a good damn. He'd earned every last one of those gray hairs the hard way.

Earned the scars, too, he acknowledged ruefully as he studied the network of fine white lines that marred the left side of his face. His left cheekbone was slightly higher than the right one, but his new nose was a decided improvement over the old model. After a few too many walk-away crashes, not to mention more barroom brawls than he cared to recall, the old one had been barely functional. This new version—he fingered the straight slope—in addition to running a true northeast, southwest course, had the added advantage of working.

Switching off the light, Brace smiled bleakly into the darkness. He'd been accused of a lot of things in his long and colorful career—of carrying a chip on his shoulder the size of an old-growth redwood. Of trying to prove something to himself—God knew what. Of running on a mixture of jet fuel, adrenaline and testosterone.

Guilty on all three counts. It had taken a fiery, near-fatal crash in the top-secret ATX-4 he'd been testing to clip his wings permanently. Thirty-two months of intermittent hospitalization for reconstruction and rehabilitation gave a man a little too much time to think.

It was during that same period that he'd met Rich Keegan. Neither man had been into socializing, but they'd had flying in common. Finding themselves alone in the ward, while the others hung out in the rec room watching TV and playing video games, they'd gradually begun to talk. Behind the protective covering of a faceful of bandages, Brace had found himself opening up for the first time since he'd confided in a foster parent some thirty-odd years before that his real father was an Air Force general who was too busy saving the world to take care of him.

Hell, he'd never had a clue as to who his old man was. His mother, either. Once, though, he'd overheard a social worker telling a cop who'd busted him for some petty offense or another that he'd been left in a shopping cart in a department store rest room and was more trouble than any kid they'd ever had to deal with.

To this day Brace could recall how proud he'd been at the distinction. They'd called him John Henry because they'd had to call him something, but he'd never felt like a John Henry. When he was thirteen, he'd taken the name of Bracewell after a local war hero who was being feted about that time. The Ridgeway had come from the department store. He'd rather liked that touch. As soon as he'd been old enough, he'd had the name made legal.

Now he wandered back out to the kitchen and lit the burner under the pot of day-old coffee. With his face in traction for so long, he'd had to give up cigarettes. Alcohol didn't mix with too many of the drugs he'd been on in the hospital, so he'd cut down on that vice, too. Mostly, he made do with bad coffee. Black as tar and strong enough to float an F-18. Sooner or later the stuff would probably eat a hole in his gut, and he'd wind up back in a hospital bed. He'd sworn never to set foot in another hospital. The day he'd walked out a free man, he'd sworn the only way anyone would ever get him back in another hospital was feetfirst, in a Ziploc bag.

He'd sworn a lot of things when he'd learned that if he so much as pulled a single G, his whole carcass would probably self-destruct.

His flying days were over, but what the hell—he'd survive. If there was one thing Brace had learned about himself over some forty-three years, it was that he was too damn mean to die young.

In the Hunt's main living room, paneled in pickled cypress and decorated with an eye more to comfort than style, he turned on the TV and slid a video in the VCR. He poured himself a pint-size mug of thick coffee and settled down to watch an old World War II training film.

The P-51. Now there was one sweet plane! Yawning, he slipped farther down into the deep leather-covered chair. The furnace cut in as the temperature fell. Outside, rain rattled against the tall windows as wind gusted against the northeast side of the house.

Half-asleep, he wondered if the woman had ever found the switch box. Probably hadn't even thought to look. Most women wouldn't know a switch box from a sushi bar. Keegan's Maudie, of course, would've had everything ticking over in two minutes flat. But then, Keegan's Maudie was one in a million.

His thoughts drifted aimlessly back to some of the women who had figured briefly in his own life over the years. By mutual choice they'd been strictly temporary diversions. Decorative, entertaining and willing.

And then, unbidden, his thoughts vectored onto a new heading, and he heard again Sharon's voice saying to someone just outside the door of his hospital room, "Oh, God, I can't stand to look at him! He can't even talk! How do they know his brain still works? What if he never looks any better than he does now? He'll have to wear a mask— Oh, God, what am I going to *tell* everybody? What am I going to *do?* No one can expect me to marry *that!*"

Sharon Bing. The sister of a man who'd been trying off and on for years to lure him into a business partnership, Sharon had been one of Pete's most effective inducements. What had started out as a casual acquaintance had unexpectedly escalated into a high-octane affair. With a background in the airline industry— old P. G. Bing had once owned a small regional airline, giving young Pete and Sharon a leg-up in the business—Sharon had liked the idea of being married to the man who had tested and helped develop one of the Navy's hottest flying machines. And Brace had thought, why not? He'd tried about everything else. Other men had taken the plunge and lived to tell the tale, so why not give it a try?

And then had come the crash. Hanging on to the ability to breathe had taken top priority for the first few weeks, but he was tougher than he'd been given credit for.

Eventually, Brace had discovered that appearances mattered a lot more to Sharon than he'd thought. She was a beautiful, brainy woman, and beautiful, brainy women could pretty much write their own ticket. He couldn't begrudge her that. He sure as hell couldn't blame her for wanting out once he no longer fit her specifications.

She'd let him down gently, he'd have to hand her that. About as gently as he'd let down the ATX-4. It had probably been the best thing that could've happened to him, he'd rationalized later. What did a guy who'd been flying solo all his life need with a wife, anyhow?

He still kept a picture of her—one of those glamour things, all heavy eyelids, pouting lips and plunging neckline, shot through a soft-focus lens. It helped to remind him, in case he was ever tempted to forget, of what could happen when a guy started taking himself too seriously.

It would've hurt a lot worse if he hadn't been groggy from all those painkillers. An unexpected side benefit of having his face ripped off and then reconstructed—getting dumped hadn't seemed all that important at the time.

Deliberately Brace pulled his thoughts out of the power dive and steered them back to the present. Which, at the moment, included a tall, skinny woman with stringy black hair, a gritty voice and the sweet disposition of a hornet with PMS.

Of course, he hadn't been all that sweet himself. But dammit, Keegan had guaranteed him complete privacy in return for keeping an eye on things for a few weeks! All he needed was a quiet, private place to hole up while he weighed his options and made his decision. How the devil could a man concentrate with a bunch of nosy strangers dropping in out of the blue, staring at his face and asking stupid questions?

Dammit, he was *not* oversensitive! He didn't give a damn what she thought, as long as she did her thinking somewhere else!

He'd give her a day, he decided. Two days, tops, but he doubted if she'd even last that long. A deserted island in late January, with the nearest shopping mall several islands away?

No way. If he knew women—and to his sorrow, he did—she'd be out of here before noon.

The old training film video droned on. Brace had watched it at least a hundred times. Yawning, he told himself he should've plugged in her phone, at least. That way she could call the marina and be out of his hair before she dug in too deeply.

First thing in the morning, just to be on the safe side, he mused drowsily, he'd run Keegan's boat around to the other side of the island, out of sight. Just in case she took it in her head not to wait for Jerry to get out of school.

"Yeah. You should be so lucky," he muttered. Yawning, he watched as the pilot of the P-51 taxied in for a perfect three-point landing, confident that no woman whose idea of a serviceable flashlight was a pink plastic gizmo the size of a lipstick tube was going to tackle a forty-horse outboard in unfamiliar waters.

Feeling the last of the tension seep out of the muscles at the back of his neck, he yawned again and told himself he might even offer to run her over himself.

Sure! Why not? And to prove what a sweetheart he was, he wouldn't even make her beg.

Two

To a woman who had mastered the word processor, the food processor, elementary plumbing and the fine art of diplomacy under fire, there was nothing particularly intimidating about an outboard motor. Frances had watched the boy from the marina punch, poke, jiggle and shove and then steer with one arm crooked casually over the handle. And while this particular model was somewhat larger, the principles were probably pretty much the same. The main thing to remember, she reminded herself, was that once she got the thing cranked up, steering was in reverse. To go right, shove the handle left and vice versa.

As a precaution, she untied the lines before she began fiddling with the controls. It had occurred to her that once she got the engine running, she might have her hands too full to worry about undoing all those fancy little knots.

A bit of common sense was called for here. Luckily, common sense was her strong suit. Thanks to her brothers, Bill and Dennis, she had a basic knowledge of combustion engines. There was nothing particularly difficult about operating an outboard engine.

Or was it a motor? Bill had explained the difference, but she'd forgotten. She'd learned to make simple repairs on most household appliances, but she could never remember the names of all the little gizmos.

Once underway, the first thing Frances noticed was that aluminum on water reacted somewhat differently than did rubber on pavement. For one thing, it lacked gripping power. By trial and error, she managed to propel the boat into open water without coming to grief, and felt a warm glow of pride.

Really, this was no big deal at all.

The second thing she noticed was the poles, which had been stuck seemingly at random along the way, one of which was green, with a light on top, the rest being plain. Not so much as a hand-painted arrow pointing the way to Coronoke or Hatteras. She'd been so tired and so intent on reaching her destination on the way over the day before that she hadn't paid them much attention.

Now, just to be on the safe side, she steered a wide course around each one. By the time it occurred to her that they might have something to do with marking a trail, every clenchable muscle she possessed was clenched, from her teeth right down to her toes. Three times she came within inches of plowing into a shoal and then had to fumble with the left-turn, right-turn thing.

Outboard motors, she decided, were designed either by or for a dyslexic. Her left-handed sister, Debbie, would have managed just fine!

As her destination drew near, it occurred to her that with no brakes except for an anchor that was stashed up under the pointy end of the boat, the good ship *Coronoke* might not be easy to park. A little test of momentum seemed indicated here. Praying she could start it again, she cut the power and carefully observed how long it took to come to a full stop.

Not too bad, she mused. But *sideways?* Where had that tricky little glide step come from? The handle was aimed straight forward.

Frances was still experimenting when her stomach began to growl, reminding her that her last meal had been a super-coronary special at a fast-food restaurant in Manteo early the previous afternoon. The fat content of all that beef, bacon and cheese alone had kept her functioning until now. However, a bowl of Fancy's Fat-Free, Fiber-Filled Homemade Granola would be her first priority once she got back to the cottage.

After two more rehearsals a safe distance away from any visible obstacles, she managed to make a creditable landing at the marina without denting either boat or pier. Still slightly terrified, but extraordinarily proud of her accomplishments—considering that the last boat she'd skippered had been a rubber affair some six inches long in a claw-footed bathtub—she tied up at the pier, briefly considered tossing out the anchor for good measure and elbowed her way up onto the splintery wharf.

And then she quietly collapsed, breathing deeply of the cold, fish-and-diesel-oil-smelling air. In the distance a noisy truck rattled past, the first sign of life she'd seen all day other than the wheeling gulls that searched the dark waters of the harbor for scraps of food.

Not until the chill began to creep into her bones did she turn to the task at hand. Making several trips to her car, she loaded her various bags and boxes aboard and set out again, her mind on trying to remember which box held her coffee filters and which held her supply of granola makings.

Somewhat to her surprise the entire operation, practice maneuvers included, had taken only slightly over an hour.

Back on Coronoke, Brace stood at the end of the pier in his briefs and boots, oblivious to the raw, cutting wind, and ran through about six yards of gutter profanity. Dammit, he'd known the first time he'd set eyes on that woman that she was going to be trouble! In the first place, she had no business even *being* here! Keegan had sworn he would have the place to himself, otherwise he never would've agreed to the deal.

Evidently she'd bought his story about the lack of basic amenities. Damn good thing, too. If that hadn't worked, he'd planned to hit her with a tale about hurricanes, tornadoes and man-eating mosquitoes and throw in a few alligators for good measure.

But dammit, why'd she have to go and steal his boat? He'd already made up his mind to ferry her back across to the marina. If there was one thing that irritated him more than a clinging, whining female, it was one of the superindependent types.

Brace had been shaving when he'd heard the outboard sputter a few times and start up. He'd gone racing down to the landing in his briefs and boots, face

covered with shaving cream, in time to see her roar out
of the harbor, hanging on to the stick like a chicken in
a high wind. While he stood there swearing, the phone
had started ringing back at the Hunt, and he'd raced
back and grabbed it just in time to hear the discon-
nect.

Still swearing under his breath, he'd jogged back
down to the landing, wondering what the devil was
happening to his nice, private little retreat. No one was
even supposed to know where he was except for the
Keegans and Pete Bing.

He figured it was Keegan, calling to check up on
things. Pete knew better than to put the screws on him
at this point in their negotiations. Brace had left it at
the "don't call me, I'll call you" stage. He still had a
lot of thinking to do before he signed on with any outfit. Not that he had any doubts about Bing Aero. He
had plenty, however, about the woman involved.

And Sharon would definitely be involved. Brace
didn't kid himself on that score. With Sharon, the
bottom line came first; personal relationships limped
in a poor second. The deal had been a straightforward
one—cash on the barrelhead in exchange for a hefty
bundle of stock in the privately owned corporation, a
modest salary and an impressive sounding title. Eventually he would take over the design division.

It was a sweet deal for a guy who had never held
down a desk in his life. Never wanted to, but now that
his choices had narrowed down, it didn't look all that
bad.

Even so, he'd have to do some pretty serious thinking before tying himself up in a long-term deal. Pete
had hinted at some of the experimental stuff they were
doing, knowing that Brace would find it hard to turn

it down, now that his test-pilot days were definitely over.

He'd been right. Brace had been up-front about the fact that he'd been approached by two other outfits and had asked for three months to make up his mind. That had been six weeks ago. The clock was still running.

And now this! Dammit, how the devil was a guy supposed to concentrate?

Scowling at the receding wake of Keegan's red runabout, he tried to recall if he'd topped off the tank after the last couple of supply runs. Late yesterday, just before she'd showed up, he'd cruised around to the northwest side of the island to check out the three hunting blinds there. He'd run over to collect his mail, and the marina had been closed, and...

Brace swore again under his breath. The lady was beginning to get on his nerves! Thanks to her tricks, he was going to have to put one of the other boats in the water and get another outboard out of storage just to retrieve the runabout.

Stalking back up to the Hunt to finish shaving and get dressed, he told himself to cheer up. At least she was gone. That was the good news.

The bad news was that he'd been the one to chase her off, and he'd lied to achieve his ends. Even at his worst he'd never been much of a liar.

Right on schedule his conscience kicked in again. Until she'd come nosing around his private sanctuary with her holier-than-thou attitude, he hadn't even known he *possessed* a conscience. So what if he hadn't exactly welcomed her to the island? Dammit, it was for her own good! She would've hated it if he'd let her stay, and he'd have had to put up with her whining about the wind and the sand and the bone-aching cold. There was nothing here for a woman. Especially not for a woman alone. Women didn't thrive in isolated outposts, they needed bright lights and lots of attention, neither of which was available on Coronoke.

And besides, dammit, she wasn't his responsibility!

On the other hand, Keegan's boat was.

Figuring she'd have had just about enough time to reach the marina if he'd left enough gas in the tank to get her that far, Brace grabbed a pass key off the board and jogged down the wooded trail to her cottage to be sure she hadn't left behind so much as a single hairpin. Once she hit Highway 12, he didn't want her to have any excuse to come back.

She hadn't left a hairpin, she'd left a whole damn suitcase! About a years' worth of supplies were still piled on the kitchen counter where he'd parked them the night before. By the time he found the toothbrush, the bottle of lotion in the bathroom and the gown tossed across the foot of her unmade bed, the tendons at the back of his neck were so tight his fingers wouldn't even uncurl.

She hadn't left. Dammit to hell and back. The miserable little sneak thief had stolen his boat and gone back for the rest of her gear! Hadn't she heard a word he'd said?

So much for the gentlemanly approach. She wanted to play hard ball? Great. Let's see how she liked his fast ball!

Working with practiced efficiency, Brace crammed her few scattered belongings into her suitcase, stripped the bed and crammed the sheets in on top of her clothes, then scanned the quarters for anything he might have missed.

He tossed her suitcase out onto the deck beside her laptop computer and stalked back inside for the groceries. She'd bought 'em—she could damn well have 'em! He only hoped she hadn't stocked up on ice cream, because he could do without having his last clean pair of jeans leaked all over!

Although in this weather, the stuff might not even have melted. The temperature hung in the low forties outside. The house, which had been battened down since October, felt even colder.

Once again the conscience Brace hadn't known he possessed kicked in. She must've worn her clothes over the nightgown to sleep in. No blanket in evidence. According to Maudie, most cottage owners provided a few summer-weight blankets, but evidently she hadn't known where to look.

"Dammit, nobody comes here in the dead of winter, especially not a lone female!" He automatically excepted Maudie Keegan, who had once lived alone on the island year-round as caretaker. Maudie was a different breed of cat. She was a local, used to the treacherous Outer Banks weather, which could go from mild to wild in a matter of minutes; accustomed to being without power, sometimes for days on end.

A small, all but unrecognizable voice whispered that maybe he should give the woman a second chance—show her around, clue her in on the power situation, lend her a few blankets and show her where to plug in her phone—

No way. She might not appreciate it now, but he was doing her a big favor. She'd probably thought she was coming down to some nice sunny beach resort where everything was laid out for her comfort, from cocktails to hot tubs.

Some travel agent somewhere needed to have his license yanked!

Brace took one last look around the cottage before locking up and heading down to the boat with her gear. It took four trips to haul it all. Good thing she hadn't come prepared for an extended stay!

But his conscience still wasn't quite ready to roll over and play dead. She'd come all the way down here, expecting the standard beach resort, and he'd more or less chased her off. It wasn't her fault—he blamed the guy who'd given her the key. Easing the small fiberglass boat away from the pier, he decided that instead of just kissing her off and good riddance, he would take the time to suggest she catch the Ocracoke ferry, and then the Cedar Island ferry, and head on down the coast until she struck summer. Jekyll Island, or maybe St. Augustine. Hell, why not go all the way to the Keys? Plenty of sunshine, plenty of company—perfect for a single woman looking for a good time.

But whatever she was looking for, she wasn't going to find it on Coronoke. Not alone. Not in January. Not while he had anything to say about it!

Frances watched as the marina receded silently in the distance. After poking and jiggling every appendage on the outboard, she had reached the inevitable conclusion that she was out of fuel. There was a single paddle in the boat, and she was wielding it as fast as she could, but it wasn't working. The harder she paddled, the faster the current carried her away from the island, and the only sign of life was seven pelicans lumbering past a few feet above the surface of the water.

Was there such a thing as carrier pelicans? Maybe she could drop a note to the Coast Guard in their pouch.

How could she have done anything so stupid! She, the practical member of the Smith family—the practical member of the Jones family, for that matter. The one who had always reminded her younger siblings to take along an umbrella and to keep enough spare change on hand to call home—the one who reminded her husband and her in-laws to take their vitamins every day and cut down on their intake of fat, sodium and refined sugar.

A small green-and-red plane droned overhead, and she stood up and waggled her arms. "Help! Down here! Send help!"

When her leather-soled loafer slipped on a patch of wet aluminum, causing the runabout to lurch, she sat down rather suddenly and gripped the sides. Really, she was beginning to feel a bit discouraged. Beginning to feel, in fact, as if she were the only living human being left on earth.

Which was absurd. She had merely run out of gas. She, who was known throughout her family for advising others never to leap without first looking, and never, *ever* to start the day without breakfast, had committed both sins, and now look at the fix she was in! Starving to death while she was being swept out to sea.

She was mentally measuring the distance to a low, marshy strip of land some thousand feet away, assessing her chances of making it to shore before she turned into an ice cube, when she became aware of a high-pitched hum, like the drone of a distant swarm of bees.

"Oh, help," she whimpered. Twisting around, she saw not one, but two boats racing toward her from opposite directions. "Thank you, Lord," she said devoutly. That water had looked awfully cold and deep and swift. "I owe you big-time for this."

As for Uncle Seymore, she had a small bone to pick with him if she ever got near a phone again. There were one or two things he'd neglected to mention concerning his precious island hideaway.

Jerry reached her first. The other boat was smaller, slower, but still headed her way at a rapid rate of speed.

"What'ja do, flood 'er?" the gangly boy called out. His lovely teeth sparkled in the pale shaft of sunlight slanting between layers of dark clouds.

"I haven't the slightest idea, but it's occurred to me that I might have run out of gas. Is that likely?"

He shrugged. Pulling alongside, he slung a line onto the runabout and stepped aboard, reaching for the red tank near the stern. Frances had never felt so stupid.

Well...yes, she had. And quite recently. But that was another story. "I'm sorry to be so much trouble. And by the way, aren't you supposed to be in school?"

Before he could answer, the other boat pulled alongside, and the same tall, scowling man who had tried to run her off the island the night before was there. She hadn't gotten a good look at his face then, but there was no mistaking that tall, rangy physique.

Embarrassed, she stole a quick glance at him. Forbidding was the first word that came to mind. Mad as the dickens was the next. And yet there was something oddly compelling about the set of his features that had nothing at all to do with his expression.

He was scowling—or maybe it was a permanent condition. It occurred to Frances that it was probably a good thing Jerry had reached her first. She wouldn't trust Flint-Face not to stuff her into a sack and throw her overboard.

"She ran outta gas," Jerry said cheerfully.

"If she'd asked before stealing my boat," Flint-Face retorted, "I would have warned her to check the levels first."

Frances resented being talked around, as if she weren't even there. "I'm sure you would," she snapped. "You warned me about everything else. As for stealing your boat, it was the only one there, and I was told there was a boat for the use of the cottagers." Without waiting for a response, she turned to the younger man. "Jerry, do you know anything about generators? Could I possibly persuade you to—"

"I'll take care of it," Flint-Face cut in. His voice reminded her of the ropes she'd used to tie up at the marina. Hard, rough, showing definite signs of wear, but none of weakness.

"Sure thing. He can check you out, ma'am. Prob'ly won't need it, though. Power's been real steady lately." He switched tanks and offered to fill the spare and leave it at the marina to be collected later, and Frances shrugged and left them to it.

At least she was no longer in danger of drifting out to sea. Jerry had thrown out an anchor, and Flint-Face kept his motor idling against the current. She waited, appreciating the sun's meager warmth on her cold backside while the two men fiddled with hoses and tanks and stainless steel fittings.

Finally Flint-Face shut off his outboard and tied his smaller boat behind her larger one, which meant, she surmised with an inward groan, that she would have the dubious pleasure of his company for the run back to the island.

Jerry veered off with a cheerful wave, sending a spray of icy water over the bow of the red runabout where Frances huddled. Sighing, she wiped the salt from her eyes. Thanks, Jerry, she thought wryly. I needed that. Having mastered so many new skills in a single morning, never mind that she'd run out of gas, her ego might have been inclined to come creeping out of hiding for the first time since she'd learned that her entire eleven-year marriage had been one giant fiasco.

"By the way, I don't believe we ever got around to introductions, did we? I'm Frances Smith Jones." She addressed the lean, rigid back, which was bent over the controls.

Silence.

Fine! If he wanted to remain anonymous, that was just fine with her. If there was one thing she was no longer interested in, it was men. Not under any circumstances. Not in *this* lifetime!

The outboard sputtered and caught again. As it settled down to a steady roar, the tall, scowling man turned and seated himself in the stern, facing her. It occurred to Frances that his eyes were exactly the color she'd always imagined an iceburg to be. Clear gray, without a glimmer of warmth. Every bit as hard as flint, if not as opaque.

As for the rest of him, it was . . . interesting, she decided. Jaw far too aggressive, cheekbones far too angular—there was something odd in the angle of them, too, but she couldn't quite put her finger on what it was. As for his mouth, at the moment it looked as if he'd just bitten into a lemon. She was tempted to smile at him, just for meanness.

His nose was beautiful. Under the pale, watery sunlight, she could see a fine network of scars on the left side of his face, but before she could even wonder about it, he said, "Ridgeway. What the hell did you think you were doing, stealing a boat when you don't even have sense enough to check the levels?"

Quite suddenly the headache she'd been ignoring all morning clamped down like a hat that was three sizes too small. Through clenched teeth, she said, "I didn't steal your boat, Mr. Ridgeway. I borrowed it. I was told on good authority that the boats were for the use of the cottage owners and renters. As for checking levels—I assume you mean the gas tank—you're right. I should have checked. Next time I will. I seldom make the same mistake twice."

He opened his mouth to speak, then shut it again and looked away. Fortunately the roar of the outboard precluded any further conversation, which gave Frances plenty of time to wonder what the luggage she had left back at the cottage was doing in the boat they were towing.

And then they swerved sharply and headed toward the marina. "Wait!" she yelled above the noise. "What are you doing? Where are you going?"

"The marina!"

"But I've already been there! I want to go back to the cottage!"

"No way, lady. Come back in a few months."

It was impossible to argue over a roaring outboard. Irked beyond bearing, her head pounding furiously, Frances crawled back to where she could make herself heard. She jammed her face as close as she dared and yelled, "Listen, I don't know what your position on Coronoke is—head jackass, at a guess—but my uncle owns that cottage, and he gave me the key and told me I could stay there until I'm good and ready to leave! It's not my fault that this Maudie person I was supposed to check in with is in Utah, but Maudie or no Maudie, I'm here to stay! So you can just damned well take me back to Coronoke right now, or I'll have you brought up on charges of—of— Well, I'll think of something!''

If he weren't so damned ticked off, Brace might have found her amusing. She wasn't as old as he'd first thought. Nor as unattractive. Although, at the moment she looked as if she'd been drawn through a keyhole backward. Opinionated women were not his favorite species, not even when they had eyes the color of bruised violets and a mouth that looked naked and vulnerable and—

Brace swore silently. Maybe he hadn't recovered as fully as he'd thought from having his broken carcass plowed into a cornfield along with several million dollars' worth of twisted metal.

Abruptly he changed direction. The woman, who'd been kneeling at his feet, yelped and would have fallen hard against the gunwale if he hadn't caught her with one arm.

Against a background of salt water and exhaust, she smelled like cut grass and flowers—sort of spicy and green. She felt like a bag of bones, even in a down-filled parka.

"Sorry," he muttered, pushing her away. He checked the boat he was towing, more as an excuse to look away from her face, which was entirely too close, than for any other reason.

Even over the roar of the outboard, he could hear the ragged intake of her breath. It occurred to him that his own was none too steady. It was a crazy reaction. He put it down to being celibate too long.

What the bloody hell had happened to all the peace and quiet he'd been promised? This place was supposed to be so far off the beaten track, nobody but duck hunters came near it between January and March. Maudie had warned him he'd be talking to Regina, the resident raccoon, before he'd been there a week. It had sounded like just what the doctor ordered.

And now, thanks to his eagerness to get rid of Ms. Smith Jones, she had about half a dozen loads of gear to haul back up to her cottage, and with his newfound conscience dogging his heels like a blasted shadow, he was going to have to offer to help her haul it.

The only bright spot on the horizon was that she obviously hated like the very devil to accept his help. Pride stuck out all over her, like quills on a porcupine. It nearly killed her to let him carry the biggest box and her overnight bag. Watching her stiff backside as she marched primly up the path before him, he almost smiled.

But not quite.

Brace knew almost as much about women as he knew about planes. During his stunt pilot days he'd been considered something of an expert. On both. It went with the territory. At the time, he'd been young enough to find studhood amusing. Without even trying, he'd collected more groupies than the star of whatever low-budget epic he happened to be stunting for, and as often as not the film's female lead headed the pack.

It had been during that period in his career that he'd met Pete and Sharon Bing, a brother-sister team who were just getting started as builders and designers of small specialty aircraft. They'd designed those special choppers for the night-fighting scene in *Killing Territory*. Sharon had let him know then she was interested, but at the time Brace had been too busy sampling what Hollywood had to offer.

After he'd left Hollywood, finished his engineering degree and started testing for a major government contractor, he'd found somewhat to his amusement that neither his bank balance nor his sex appeal had suffered to any great degree. But by then he'd been older and a lot more selective. By then, too, the world had become a more dangerous place.

That was about the time when Sharon Bing had reentered his life. They'd started going out together. After three months he'd asked her to marry him. Or she'd asked him. Later he was never sure which one of them had brought it up. But the sex had been good, which made two vital interests they'd shared.

It wouldn't have lasted past the honeymoon. They'd already had that. Some men were husband material— some weren't. Now, thanks to his recently remodeled physiognomy, he no longer had to worry about it. Most women were turned off by his scars, but a few were turned on in a way that made him angry and uncomfortable. It never seemed to occur to either type that in spite of some extensive reconstruction, he was still the same man inside. Not that he'd ever pretended to be any great bargain.

"One more trip," the tall brunette announced as she set the first load down on the screened front deck. "I can handle the rest, thanks."

He hadn't offered. Now, perversely, he insisted. "I'll get the rest," he growled. "Go inside and get warm."

"First, I'm afraid you'll have to show me how the generator works. I don't want to risk another disaster so soon. I usually try to hold it down to one a day."

The generator. "Look, lady—ma'am—Ms. Jones—"

"Frances. Frances Smith Jones."

"Right. Look, about the generator, you don't need to bother. The power's working now." Actually, there hadn't been a full power outage since he'd arrived on the island. A few blinks and a brownout or two when the wind kicked up. Tough on compressors, but as everything on the island was rigged with trip-out switches, it was no major deal. "All you have to do, Ms. Jones, is throw the breaker. The box is behind that door. You want me to do it for you?"

His arms were crossed over his chest, and so were hers. It occurred to Brace to wonder if she was as skilled at reading body language as he was, and for some reason the notion amused him.

She stood her ground like a veteran, though. He'd give her full marks for guts.

"I'm perfectly capable of dealing with a switch box, Mr. um... But perhaps you'd better show me about the generator just in case."

"They're only used for backup. You won't be here long enough to need it."

An arc welder couldn't have thrown off any more sparks than her eyes did. Blue fire. Lavender blue fire. Unfortunately, to a man who'd made a career of living dangerously, it was a sure turn-on.

Brace took two steps back, his own eyes growing wary. Oh, no. No way was this woman going to get to him, lavender blue eyes, long legs, wide, soft, vulnerable mouth or not. He needed a woman right now like he needed another hole in his head.

Or another plate in his skull.

"Let me know when you're ready to pack it in, Ms. Jones. I'll run you over to the marina. That way we'll both be sure you get there in one piece," he said, one hand on the doorknob.

Frances smiled sweetly. "You're too kind," she said through clenched teeth as he quietly closed the door.

Kind. Yeah. Sure he was.

Three

————

By evening the clouds had moved in again. The wind howled like a roomful of tomcats, but at least the rain held off. Frances gulped down two more aspirin, eyed the sacks of staples still waiting to be put away and decided that if her sinuses didn't stop giving her fits, she was going to trade them in on a new set. Evidently, salt air and ocean breezes weren't quite the panacea they were cracked up to be.

And another thing—she'd always heard that being on the water was a terrific appetizer. One more old wives' tale shot to blazes. Her stomach kept telling her it was hungry, but when she offered to feed it, it rebelled on her. Nice going for a professional dietician. She couldn't even tempt her own palate.

Maybe her headache had put her off her feed. The trouble was she needed to get started on proofing the copy she'd brought with her for Fancy's Kitchen, her monthly cooking column—the last column she would write before her resignation took effect—and she couldn't even bring herself to do that.

As for working on *Fancy's Fat-Free Favorites*, her collection of low-fat recipes, she was already two weeks past her deadline. If she didn't wrap it up and get it into her editor's hands soon, the market would be flooded with low-fat cookbooks and her publisher would find a loophole in her contract and make her return her modest advance.

Her *extremely* modest advance. And she needed the money. She'd received a third on signing the contract, with another third promised once the final manuscript was approved, and the last to be paid on publication. She'd been so thrilled when they'd accepted her proposal—she'd only sent it in because her editor at the magazine had pushed her to do it. He'd liked the idea of having a published author doing his food column, and Frances had liked the idea of anything that would take her mind off her dismal home life.

And now here she was, with nothing but time on her hands—no carping demands, no whining complaints, no dirty dishes, unmade beds and un-run errands waiting for her attention the minute she stepped through the front door. No reason at all not to dig in and get the job done, other than that she felt like the very devil.

Maybe she could sell her publisher on another idea— *Fancy's Recipes From Hell.*

By evening she hadn't seen a single soul. Evidently, she and Flint-Face were the only two people on the island. Not a particularly happy thought. What was his name, anyway? Racetrack? Railway? Bridgeman?

Whatever.

Frances had never been particularly gregarious—
actually, she'd never had time to consider whether she
was or wasn't—but she wasn't exactly a hermit, either.
The eldest of five children, she was used to being surrounded by people. Her mother had died when she was
seventeen, and Frances had been forced to curtail her
own modest social life, postpone her plans to enroll at
the university and settle for day classes at the local
community college for the first few years.

Not that she'd regretted it for a single moment. At
least, not after her initial disappointment. Home had
always been a noisy, cheerful place, constantly over-
run with family, friends and friends of friends.

Some of them very special friends, she thought in a
rare mood of nostalgia as she stirred herself a cup of
cocoa, set it aside untouched and drifted across to stare
out the dark window. Twice—once when she was
eighteen and again when she was twenty-one—she had
come that close to getting engaged. By that time, her
father, a research scientist involved in a lifelong love
affair with the parasitic plants of various tropical
regions, had more or less abandoned them.

Oh, financially they'd been secure enough, except
for the threat of ever-rising property taxes. The house
had been paid for, Frances had always been an excellent manager, and they'd all found after-school jobs as
soon as they'd gotten old enough. But as long as her
father had remained out of the country—and he'd
shown no signs of coming back home—they'd remained her responsibility. A package deal, as she'd
laughingly told Paul, a fellow day student who had
been on the verge of proposing at the time.

He hadn't. Instead, he'd started going out with her
best friend, Carol, and when Carol had discovered she

was pregnant, Paul had suddenly found it necessary to check out a job offer on the West Coast. He had never written, never called, never returned. Frances had been with Carol when her baby was born. She'd done her best to console her after she'd put it up for adoption, still feeling guilty for having introduced her to Paul in the first place, but secretly relieved at having escaped herself.

Three years later she had felt obliged to warn another contender. The children were older by then. She'd finally been able to transfer her few transferable credits to the university, but she was still the acting head of the family. So she'd told Adam about her absentee father and seventeen-year-old Debbie and sixteen-year-old Reba and the twins, Bill and Dennis, because Adam was mature enough to appreciate family responsibility. He was entirely different from Paul. A lawyer with political interests, he was older, more serious, and besides, they were head over heels in love, which was why he'd been able to talk her into moving out of the dormitory and into his apartment.

Duly warned, Adam had decided that, while he was still more than willing to share his apartment—and incidentally, his bed—it would be a bad career move at this point in his life to saddle himself with a family.

Frances remembered smiling until she thought her face would break, furious with herself for being so blind. Twice she had fallen in love. Twice she had given her trust. Both times she'd been dropped at the first hurdle, her confidence in her own judgment badly shaken.

Learning to trust again hadn't been easy, but four years later, as a newly graduated nutritionist employed at a small private hospital, she had met Kenneth Jones. The first thing that had impressed her was the fact that he seemed so devoted to his parents. Her own family by that time had outgrown the dependent stage, but she'd been forced by circumstances into a position of responsibility for too many years. It had become a habit.

Her father, had he still been alive, would have appreciated Kenneth, she thought with bitter amusement. She hadn't known until it was far too late how much her late husband had in common with the parasitic plants Dr. Smith had spent the last years of his life studying.

"Oh, this is depressing!" she muttered. Why in the world was she wasting time wallowing in past misery?

Refocusing her mind on her current misery, Frances swallowed a few gulps of the lukewarm cocoa and forced down a slice of toast. Her stomach threatened rebellion. Change of water, she told herself. Or too much greasy junk food on the trip down. There were times when she devoutly wished she didn't know beans about food. There came a time in every woman's life when she desperately needed to indulge herself in something utterly wicked, even if it was no more than an overdose of saturated fat, refined sugar, bleached flour and a bushel basketful of assorted chemicals.

At the moment, however, not even the thought of forbidden fruit could tempt her. She felt utterly lousy!

The next day started off with a bang—with a series of bangs—and plummeted from there. The explosions began just after daybreak, and Frances sat up in bed, heart thundering, brain still foggy, thinking she was still in the middle of a nightmare. Prying open one eye, she focused it blearily on her alarm clock. Both hands dangled straight down. Either the thing was broken, or it was only five-thirty, or she'd forgotten to change it when she'd left Indiana.

Or all of the above. God, at this time of year, five-thirty was practically the middle of the night!

"Go 'way," she moaned. Falling back, she piled a pillow over her head, but it didn't help. The barrage continued. After a while she gave up. It was dark as pitch outside, her head was splitting, someone had turned up the heat, and World War III was being conducted right outside her bedroom window.

Groaning, she trotted out a few rusty four-letter words, left over from her college days. Which also didn't help. Even if she'd had a phone, she wouldn't have known whether to call the police or the national guard.

Or an ambulance. She felt perfectly awful! She almost wished they'd shoot her and get it over with!

Feeling more miserable than she'd ever felt in her life—at least since she'd overdosed on chocolate-covered cherries after Adam's defection—she splashed water on her face and pulled on the clothes she had thrown across the foot of the bed the night before. Maybe it was just a delayed reaction from the wretched mess she'd been going through for the past few weeks, she told herself.

Make that the past few years.

The gunfire was sporadic now, but every brief burst rattled painfully against her skull. Her stomach wouldn't tolerate any more aspirin, but she didn't have anything else, and she was reasonably certain there was no pharmacy on this scruffy, miserable island.

Oh, Lord, she was whining. She *hated* whiners! Forcing her body to move, she dragged on her parka and stumbled to the door. If she was going to die all alone and unmourned, she'd better leave word with old Flint-Face where to ship the remains. Debbie would want to know that their mother's silver was now officially hers. Reba already had the piano, and the twins...

She swallowed her nausea and lurched toward the far end of the island.

Brace was awake when the shooting started. He'd been halfway expecting it ever since the weather had closed in. Keegan had warned him that a few hunters who'd been coming down to Coronoke for years for the duck hunting, still did. Evidently their grandfathers had been members of the original hunt club, and a small thing like a change of ownership didn't signify. Rather than make an issue of it, the Keegans tolerated it, knowing the blinds wouldn't last much longer, and they wouldn't be permitted to rebuild.

He should have warned the Jones woman, though. He'd thought about it, decided it would serve her right and then had forgotten all about it. Now, dammit, he was feeling guilty again. This conscience business was getting to be a royal pain in the rudder!

He had just stepped out of the shower when someone banged on his front door. Lady Blackbeard, no doubt. An unholy smile lit his eyes as he ran through several possibilities. If he'd wanted to be rid of her—and God knows he did—this just might do the trick. All he had to do was let her think the worst.

Which would be...what? Drug wars? She'd hardly believe a drive-by shooting. A sail-by shooting? A turf war? Hatfields versus McCoys, island-style? Now there was a possibility. In fact, all he had to do was keep his trap shut, and odds were her own imagination would do the rest. She'd be out of here before the dew was off the dandelions.

Knotting the towel around his hips, Brace stepped into his boots. Nudity was one thing, bare feet another. If that made him a tenderfoot, he could live with that.

"Yeah, yeah, okay," he grumbled. Trying not to grin, he swung the door open. Come to think of it, wasn't there supposed to be a bombing range somewhere out in the sound? He might just drop a few hints about war games while he was at it.

One look at the woman clinging to the doorframe and he forgot about games of any kind. She looked like hell warmed over. Her crushed-violet eyes were stained with pain, her face was unnaturally flushed, and she was shaking so hard her teeth rattled.

Without a word he took her by the arm and hauled her inside. "Come on—easy now, it's not that bad." His narrowed eyes searched her face. She wasn't a pretty woman, not by his standards. Striking, maybe. Even handsome. Great bone structure, only a little too much of it was visible. She could do with a few added pounds.

"Need to borrow your phone," she rasped.

"This is about more than the duck hunters, right?"

"Duck hunters? At five-thirty in the morning?"

"Six-thirty. Eastern Standard."

Frances closed her eyes and swayed on her feet, and Brace grabbed her again before she could topple over against Maudie's easel. "You'd better sit down and tell me what's wrong. You don't look so hot." He steered her toward Keegan's massive leather-covered chair, and she collapsed, looking pale and flushed at the same time. Not a reassuring combination.

Right on cue his damned conscience elbowed him in the gut, and reluctantly he knew he had to play it straight with her. "Look, it's not as bad as it sounds. I guess I should've warned you about these guys—they come down here a few times during the season from somewhere up in Virginia—just a harmless bunch of businessmen. They'll bag their limit, booze up a little to keep warm and then head on back up the beach. Noisy, but no real threat." His narrowed eyes searched her finely drawn features. "But that's not what's bugging you, right?"

"Phone . . . please?"

Without a word he brought her the phone. Some cottages hadn't yet gotten around to having them installed. Of those that had, some were kept locked up along with the cottage owner's personal gear to prevent misuse by renters. He didn't know which category she fell into. At the moment it didn't matter.

She reached out, but her hand was trembling so hard she was having trouble punching out the numbers. "Better let me dial for you. Want to give me the number?" He wasn't even sure she had enough strength to carry on a conversation.

"Doctor first. Then sister . . . ah, area code 219 . . ." Her eyes were closed, and Brace felt something he hadn't felt in a long time. In about thirty-five years, to be exact. She looked like hell and obviously felt worse, but he had a sneaking suspicion those hollows under her elegant cheekbones and the shadows around her eyes hadn't happened overnight.

Ignoring her feeble protest, he quickly dialed the number of the closest medical facility, handed her the

phone and watched as she pulled herself together. She
was hanging in there, he'd have to hand her that.

"Frances Jones—I'm staying in the Seymore cottage on Coronoke," she said hoarsely. Brace listened
openly as she listed her symptoms. Long before she was
done, he'd made his own diagnosis. Fortunately he'd
had his flu shots before he'd left the hospital.

"Yes, I—" she said, and then, after a long pause,
"No, I can't come to the— Well, yes, I understand,
but—"

There were several more *buts,* and then Brace removed the phone from her weak grasp and briefly
outlined the situation. By the time he hung up, he was
cursing the system, cursing the weather and cursing the
luck that had landed him with a sick woman on his
doorstep when all in the world he wanted was to be left
alone.

But for all his shortcomings—and God knew they far
outnumbered his longcomings—he wasn't a man to
turn his back on need. And at the moment the lady was
about as needy as they came.

Frances opened her eyes to the awful memory of
having been violently sick more than once. Of having
someone hold her head up, shove a bucket in her face
and then mop her off. Of throwing off her covers and
freezing and then burning up and being mopped off
again.

She had no idea what other indignities she had suffered. She was wearing a nightgown, and it was dry,
and she distinctly remembered being wet. She remembered, now that she thought about it, that she'd been
fully dressed when she'd gone to make a phone call.

Cautiously she opened one eye. It hurt, but it still worked, after a fashion. Which meant she was alive. So far, so good. Her head still ached, but it no longer felt as if it were the size of a blimp, and while she felt queasy and weak, she wasn't actively nauseated.

Broken bits of memory filtered in, and she grimaced. Had Flint-Face really done all those ikky things for her that she'd done for the children when they were growing up and catching everything that went through school?

Somewhere a door opened, and she experimented with opening both eyes at once. For the first time she realized that she was not in her own bed in Blackbeard's Pit or Lair or whatever. She hadn't been there long enough to feel at home, but she did know that this long, narrow room with the high ceiling and the dark, paneled walls was not where she was supposed to be sleeping.

"Feel like something to drink?"

Blearily she watched as he approached the bed. He was carrying a tray with a cup and a can of cola. He looked eight feet tall and utterly intimidating to a woman who was horizontal and still wondering how she'd come to be that way.

"You lost a lot of fluid."

"Oh, Lord," she mumbled miserably.

"Tea or cola? You feel like crackers? Doc said try you with crackers first and then toast, and as soon as you can keep those down, he'll send over something for your head. I expect it feels like the devil."

Her mouth tasted like cotton, only worse. Her hair felt limp and sticky—she felt sticky all over. How ironic to have nursed everything from mumps to malingering, from head lice to hypochondria, in others, without ever having been sick a day in her life—or rather, never having had time to give in to it. Now here she was, laid low at the worst possible time, under the worst possible circumstances.

"I'm so sorry," she whispered, trying to sound firm and failing miserably.

"Don't be. It happens."

"Not to me, it doesn't."

He lifted both eyebrows, and Frances noticed for the first time that along with the faint silvery network of scars on the left side of his face, there was a deeper scar running diagonally through one eyebrow, which lent him a distinctly rakish look. "Cast-iron constitution?" he suggested with a crooked smile.

Amazing what a difference a smile made. She found herself wanting to hang all over him and pour out her troubles on his accommodating shoulders—which only proved that her mind, as well as her stomach, had been affected by whatever evil spell she'd fallen under.

"Too busy," she managed. She felt like weeping and told herself it was only a temporary weakness. She never cried. "You've been awfully decent about this—about—" She gestured helplessly. Men weren't comfortable around sick people. She suspected his type of man—not that she'd ever run across his particular subspecies before—would thoroughly detest it. "Whatever it was," she rasped. "But I'm over it now. I'd better get out of your way."

"Don't even think about moving." He set the tray on the bedside table, an ornate affair of marble and mahogany with big, curly feet. "You'd get rolled by the first puff of wind. Hush up now, and let me play doctor, okay? I'm just beginning to get the hang of it."

Remembering the phone call she'd made just before the world spun out on her, Frances grumbled, "That Doctor What's-his-name wouldn't even prescribe over the phone, even though he said he was pretty sure he knew what ailed me." Frowning, she remembered standing up too quickly, and then the floor had tilted and...

Suddenly she had a very definite impression she'd be happier not remembering anything more.

"Let me help you sit up," he said as he slid an arm under her shoulders before she could protest. The moment his large, warm hands slid under her back, she began to tremble. "Cold? Your fever broke about ten this morning, but Doc said to watch out for a delayed chill."

"This m-m-morning? Thank goodness! I was afraid I'd b-b-been here for days—it feels like it."

"Only a day and a night. You were down for the count most of—"

"A day and a night!" she squawked. "But how did I— Who—"

"Hey, don't sweat it, okay? I put you to bed and then retrieved enough gear from your place to change you when you needed it. No big deal."

She covered her face and moaned. "If you don't mind, I think I'd prefer to die now." She had never been so embarrassed in her life. It was one thing for a stranger to hold a bucket while she was sick—that was bad enough. But for that same stranger to undress her and change her nightgown and...

Oh, for pity's sake, no one had ever done that for her, not even Kenneth, in all the years she'd been married to him before he'd died.

Planting one knee on the bed beside her, Brace lifted her up, his arm supporting her back. When her head toppled over onto his shoulder, he discovered that it was altogether different from holding a semiconscious woman while she cast up her accounts.

It occurred to him that since Frances Smith Jones, with her long, elegant bones, her ivory velvet skin and her crushed violet eyes had invaded his sanctuary, he was discovering a lot of things about himself he'd never even suspected. For a guy who'd never even owned a pet—at least not in some thirty-five years, since his pet rat, Simon, had pigged out on arsenic-laced cheese—he hadn't done a half-bad job of care giving.

Not bad at all...

By evening, Frances was feeling almost human. It occurred to her that she'd probably been ripe for the first virus to come along. She'd been running flat out for years with her job as food editor and columnist for a small regional magazine, plus working on the book that was supposed to make her reputation and augment her skimpy wages, and taking care of the house and her demanding in-laws.

And then, a few days before Christmas, her whole life had crumbled in a single moment when she'd stumbled on to something the whole town had known for years—that practically from the beginning, she'd been sharing her husband with another woman! And as if that weren't enough, his parents—sweet, elderly Florence and Henry Jones, who had moved into the spare bedroom because they were afraid to live alone— the pair she had waited on hand and foot and listened to until her ears ached, catered to and supported both physically and financially until she was worn to a frazzle—had known all along about their son's double life!

At first she'd refused to believe it. The denial stage, according to Carol, who had read a lot of pop psychology after the thing with Paul and the baby. Next had come the anger and then the determination to cut every single tie with the past and start fresh somewhere else, as far away as possible.

Which was probably just another form of denial. Only by then she'd been far too furious to worry about labels.

For two years Frances had dutifully mourned her late husband, refusing to admit, even though her marriage had long since settled into a hollow routine, that she'd made a bad mistake in her choice of a mate.

Refusing to admit that, once again, she had misplaced her trust.

Throwing off the shackles of the past had not been easy to arrange, especially for someone who was accustomed to shouldering responsibility. By then the Joneses had entangled their lives so deeply with hers that she'd had to hack her way free, sacrificing some things that might have been salvaged. Numbly she'd packed up her personal belongings, seen her lawyer and signed over the house. Let Florence and Henry worry about payments, insurance, maintenance and taxes for a change! Let them worry about keeping the neighbor's yapping dog quiet so they could sleep and seeing that the paperboy left the paper on the porch instead of on the roof. Let them worry about—

Oh, drat! The trouble was, she thought now, she'd been running on sheer nerves for so long it was little wonder that the first time she'd slowed down, some wretched little virus had caught up with her.

Brace held her stiff, huddled form in his arms, watching with a quizzical look as her delicate jaw firmed and her eyes began to send off sparks. "Gonna keep it down, or shall I grab the bucket again?"

Frances had to laugh, even as the tears of weakness and frustration threatened to overflow. "Did anyone ever compliment you on your bedside manner?"

Touched by the valiant effort she was making when she obviously felt like the devil, he grinned. "No, and I won't hold my breath."

"I'm fine. Thank you," she tacked on belatedly. It occurred to her that her own manners could stand some improvement. The trouble was she wasn't used to being on the receiving end of anyone's care giving.

Stuffing the pillows behind her back, he stepped away, waited to see if she was going to topple over and, when she didn't, left her. As she watched his back disappear through the doorway, the tears spilled over, and she sniffled, gulped and mopped her face with the sleeve of her gown.

This is utterly disgusting, she told herself. She had to get out before she made a complete fool of herself—if it wasn't already too late. Grimacing, she sipped the cola and nibbled half a cracker, not because she wanted it, but because she needed her strength.

The clothes she'd been wearing were hanging neatly in the big mahogany wardrobe beside several pairs of jeans and an assortment of drab shirts. Gray knit, black flannel and one the color of blackstrap molasses. Holding on to the bedpost, she managed to get herself dressed. It took almost more strength than she possessed, but determination helped out. Finally, swaying in the living room doorway, she rehearsed what she wanted to say.

He was reading. Light from the tall window shone cruelly down on his angular features, highlighting the irregularity of his cheekbones and the tracery of scars along the left side of his face.

Taking a steadying breath, Frances launched into her prepared bread-and-butter speech. "Mr. Bridgeman, you've been very decent about all this, and you were certainly under no obligation. Thank you very—"

"Ridgeway."

"What?" Under several layers of pink nylon and periwinkle wool, she was freezing. Her voice quavered. She was shaking all over.

"It's Brace Ridgeway, and dammit, you're not supposed to be up!" He unfolded his lanky frame from the armchair and stalked across the room, no pretense of any bedside manner in evidence.

Frances clutched the bundle of nightclothes, bedding and the few toilet articles he had brought over from her cottage. "Mr. Ridgeway, I'm fully recovered now, thanks to your excellent nursing, so I'll just get on back to my own place and let you have your bed back."

"Keep it. I put you there because it was the only one made up."

"Yes, well—thank you again, but I think it would be better if I—"

"Judas priest, lady, quit trying to be so damned independent! You're not up to thinking yet."

If she'd needed something to stiffen her spine, that did the trick. "It may come as a surprise, but I've been doing my own thinking for a number of years now. It's become something of a habit. So thank you very much, and I'll return your linens as soon as they're washed and dried."

He hurled the book he was holding onto an over-stuffed hassock. "Go ahead then, have a relapse! See if I care! I never invited you here in the first place. And in case nobody ever told you, you've got a lousy attitude, Jones!"

Later Frances would think of any number of stinging retorts. At the moment all she could think of was getting away before she started crying again. She *never* cried! It was just one more stupid symptom of what ailed her—the Carolina weeping flu, at a guess—but if she cried now, he'd think it was because of him, and no man would ever have that kind of power over her again.

"Fine," she said with admirable poise. "And thank you again for everything, Mr. Ridgeway. I'll leave your bed linens on the table on my porch when they're done. You may collect them at your convenience."

It took the last dregs of stamina she possessed, but she marched past him with her chin up, her eyes dry and her knees scarcely even wobbling.

So her vision was a little blurred, and there was a lump the size of a loaf of bread in her throat. She wasn't actually crying. Crying never accomplished a blessed thing—unless you were Florence Jones, and then it accomplished plenty!

And what was wrong with her attitude, anyway? Wait until *he* came down with the weeping, aching, stomach-rebelling flu. Then we'd see how well *his* attitude fared!

Four

Her brief burst of energy short-lived, Frances slept for most of the day. She woke up late in the afternoon, starved and feeling sticky. By the time she had soaked, shampooed her hair and lotioned every inch of her aching body, noting morosely as she did so that her bones were more prominent than ever, she was hungry, but too tired to eat.

Her kitchen hadn't magically cleaned itself in her absence. The same cup, half-filled with cold, curdled cocoa, sat on the table. The same sack of groceries sat on the counter. The same manuscript, waiting to be completed, proofed and recopied, was set out neatly beside her laptop, along with a jumble of notes on possible additions and amendments and her final column.

Copied? Oh, great. One more thing she hadn't thought through when she'd burned her bridges behind her. Her editor at the magazine had been convinced that with the publication of her cookbook, her readership, and thus his, would double. On the basis of that he had generously allowed her the use of an office computer, including a laser printer, to make up for the fact that he paid peanuts for the two monthly columns she did.

To think she was the one who had always preached looking before leaping, Frances thought ruefully. She'd never been able to afford impulsiveness, which was probably a good thing as she obviously didn't do it particularly well.

It was while she was putting away the staples she'd bought on the way south that Brace Ridgeway rapped on her door and let himself in. It hadn't occurred to her to lock it. The island was practically uninhabited, after all, and she'd have had to dig out the key. And sooner or later, the way her luck had been running lately, she would have locked herself out.

"Did I forget and leave something behind?" she asked. She was wearing an ancient nightshirt and a red flannel bathrobe, and while she wasn't exactly dressed for entertaining, he had seen her in less. Remembering just how much less, she felt the hot color rush to her cheeks.

He came inside the door and stopped, as if ready to bolt. His big leather jacket hung open over baggy jeans, and his streaky, dark blond hair, obviously styled by the wind, brushed his sheepskin collar. "What do you think you're doing now?" he demanded suspiciously.

"Answering stupid questions."

"Don't get smart with me."

"Then don't ask stupid questions."

"I brought you your supper. I figured you'd sleep all day."

"I did. And thank you very much, but I'm perfectly capable of making my own supper."

"Yeah? Is that why you look like you're about to keel over? Lady, for your information, you lost a lot of strength yesterday. A few saltines and a couple of shots of cola aren't enough to make up the difference. I brought soup."

Soup. Her mouth watered. She had won blue ribbons for her own chicken-lemon soup. Her beef, egg and noodle soup had won her a monstrous silver bowl, suitably engraved.

Of course, her mother-in-law had turned up her nose when she'd discovered that it was only silver plate, but as Frances had told her at the time, it was the thought that counted. And right now her thoughts were focused on soup. Hot, rich, tasty, homemade.

Slowly, reality began to set in. "What kind of soup?"

"I brought over a couple of cans. It's your call."

"It's canned?"

"Lady, do I look like Julia Child to you?"

"Sorry, I wasn't thinking."

"I thought that was one of your habits."

"Apologizing?"

"Thinking."

It took a while for her to catch up with him. When she did, remembering their earlier confrontation, the last of her strength deserted her and she dropped down onto a chair, shoulders sagging. "Do you suppose we could skip over the past few days and start all over again?"

Brace shrugged, trying not to notice her ankles, which looked almost too delicate to bear her weight. She was barefooted. Her feet were long and slender, the toenails innocent of polish. For a skinny broad, her calves were surprisingly well turned, and as for her knees, where her robe fell apart...

His imagination tripped into automatic, and he ruthlessly yanked the plug. Digging the two cans of generic brand soup from the pockets of his sheepskin-lined flight jacket, he slammed them down on the countertop. "Don't you own a pair of slippers?"

"I happen to like going barefooted."

"In *January?* Lady, you need a keeper, you know that? How the hell did you manage to survive all these years?"

"By avoiding overbearing jerks who use the word *lady* as if it were an insult."

They glared at each other. Frances experienced a momentary flashback to the twins' favorite argument from puberty through adolescence. The standard dialogue consisted solely of a series of "Yeah" and "Oh, yeah," and lasted until someone—usually Frances— stepped in and broke the impasse.

At the thought, the corners of her lips twitched. Her eyes began to sparkle in her wan face, and Brace tipped his head to one side.

"You feeling okay?" He fixed her with a suspicious glare. "You're not about to crack up or anything, are you?" Edging toward the door, he looked ready to run for cover at the first sign of danger.

"Sorry. I wasn't smiling at you, I was smiling at my twin brothers."

He blinked. His split-level left eyebrow went a little crazy, and then he said, "Yeah. Right."

Which, for some reason, sent her into gales of laughter. At his look of alarm, she tried to explain, but by the time she could manage a halfway coherent explanation, her guest chef was rummaging through the kitchen drawers in search of a can opener.

"Tomato's not bad with a shot of tabasco, but if you think it'll be too rough on your stomach, there's split pea. Take your pick."

A couple more deep breaths and she had herself under control, except for her watering eyes and the fact that she felt limp as a raw egg. "It sounds lovely," she said. Leaning back, she let her lids fall shut, too tired to care as long as she didn't have to move a muscle in the foreseeable future.

Besides, as long as she appeared helpless, he didn't seem quite so wary, and Frances discovered that she didn't want to scare him off—not just yet.

"What sounds lovely? You mean both?"

"Why not?" she asked, without opening her eyes. "Mix 'em up, add a little sherry and we'll call it a bisque."

"You're serious?"

Her eyes opened and she stared at him, intrigued by the odd, self-deprecating gentleness that kept cropping up each time his mask of toughness slipped. "I never joke about food," she said gravely. "Food is serious business."

He gave her a wary look and then shrugged again. Judging from his height and the width of his shoulders, he should weigh in the neighborhood of two hundred pounds. He probably didn't even come up to one seventy. Had he been ill? Had he been in an accident? Didn't he have anyone to look after him and see that he ate properly?

Speaking of habits, she thought wryly, the habit of taking care of every stray in the neighborhood was definitely one she was going to have to break. He was none of her business, and besides, she was too tired. There was only one really comfortable chair in the house, and she was in it. And as long as someone fed her at fairly regular intervals, she just might stay there until she grew moss on her north side. "Mr. Ridgeway—Brace—I really don't care what you do with it or what you call it, just so long as you don't expect me to do more than lift a soup spoon."

She heard the grind of a can opener and the clatter of pans. Her kitchen would probably qualify for Federal disaster aid by the time he finished the simple task. So be it. She honestly didn't remember the last time anyone had catered to her needs, not even after she'd fractured her left wrist trying to turn Mother Jones's mattress for the fourth time in a single day. Mother Jones suffered, from among several other phantom ailments, the Princess and the Pea syndrome.

"Got any sherry?" Brace asked.

Her eyes blinked open, and Frances found herself face-to-thigh with her impromptu chef. Startled face to lean, muscular thigh. She sat up and drew in a deep, steadying breath. He smelled like leather and laundry detergent. "Sherry?" she repeated.

"For the OD special I'm whipping up. What'd you call it, brisk?"

"Bisque. OD as in overdose?"

"OD as in olive drab. You ever seen the color of this stuff? You might want to eat it with your eyes closed, in case it brings on a relapse."

"Orange and green make...mud. I hadn't thought about the color, and no, I don't have any sherry. If

Uncle Seymore has any, it's under lock and key. I wasn't really serious, you know.''

He rolled his eyes heavenward. They were actually rather nice eyes, she told herself. Still wary, but at the moment, more like rain than ice.

"Now she tells me," he muttered. Reaching over to turn off the burner, he said, "Don't start without me. Be right back."

Feeling sleepy, hungry and slightly bemused, Frances allowed her eyelids to drift shut again. Back in Fort Wayne in her tiny test kitchen, she had once made blue corn bread and served it with yellow tomato jam. She could handle a bowlful of olive drab soup if she had to.

Come to think of it, she could probably handle *two* bowlfuls. Easily. Suddenly she was starved!

Brace was back within minutes, a teacup in his hand. With a quick glance at where she lay sprawled in the big leather chair—she hadn't so much as moved a muscle since he'd been gone—he crossed to the stove and dumped the contents into the stockpot.

She sniffed. Her brow wrinkled. "Sherry?"

"Bourbon," he said, and her eyes flew open.

"Bourbon—*whiskey?*"

"It'll put a little iron in your blood. Smells pretty good, if I do say so myself. Maybe I missed my calling."

Frances didn't ask how much whiskey had been in that teacup. She didn't want to know. She never drank more than the occasional glass of wine; not from any prohibitionist leanings, but because it was an expensive habit she could easily do without.

He served her soup on a tray, and she poked at the thick mixture with her spoon. "If swamp gas had a color, this would be it," she said as she cautiously tasted it. Brace waited, his face registering a disarming blend of hope and wariness. "Mmm. Strange, but interesting," she said, and then tried a larger sample. "In fact, *very* interesting."

He heaved a sigh of relief and ladled another bowlful. "Yeah, I sorta thought it might be a pretty good combination."

Frances shot him a skeptical look. "Sure, you did. An old family favorite, Brace's Best Bourbon Brisk, handed down through generations of Ridgeways, right?"

Eyes strangely shuttered, he ignored the remark. After a few minutes he said, "But the bourbon adds a little something, doesn't it?"

"Roughly double the calories, for starters. It takes more cooking time than most people realize to burn off alcohol."

They ate in silence for a few minutes, and then he got up and rummaged in the bread box until he found a box of store-bought soda biscuits. "Got anything with salt on it?" he asked.

"No, and you don't need anything with salt on it. There's enough sodium in this stuff for a family of five." She spoke without thinking, conditioned by years of dealing with diets in one circumstance or another. "You said you missed your calling. What is your calling, anyway?"

"Test pilot," he said brusquely, and her spoon clattered against her tray.

"Test pilot! I should have guessed."

"Why?"

"Well, I suppose it takes a certain reckless disregard for life and limb to even think of stirring up an incendiary mixture like this." Unexpectedly she grinned.

Watching the way her eyes lit up, her companion entertained the passing thought that skinny women with angular jawlines and high, hollow cheeks weren't exactly plain. After all, the combination hadn't done Katherine Hepburn much harm, he mused.

"Seconds?" he asked, rising.

She held out her empty bowl. "Since I'm not driving, I don't mind if I do."

There was a little more conversation the second time around, although Frances couldn't help but feel as if Brace was still on guard. As if he didn't quite trust her.

What's not to trust? she wondered, half-amused. She was feeling remarkably improved—although she'd just as soon not know how much of that improvement was due to nourishment and how much to the bourbon—but she was certainly no threat to anyone.

Brace had turned off the overhead light in the kitchen area and switched on a table lamp, and in the oblique light, she studied him quite boldly. Which had to be due to the bourbon, because soup had never affected her this way before.

From the neck up, she decided, he looked like a collection of spare parts. The thought amused her, and she smiled a lazy, contented smile. From the neck down, he could use some fattening up. Cream-based soups, rich pastries—all the things any sensible person would avoid like the plague. Her gaze strayed down over his chest, which was surprisingly convex under the black flannel shirt. His hips were negligible, but somehow she had a feeling there was more to him than appeared on the surface.

When she caught him watching her watching *him*, she felt the beginnings of a hot flush that had nothing at all to do with premature menopause. "Remind me not to go near alcohol again, will you?" she muttered, more amused than alarmed. She hadn't thought about men in *that* particular context in years!

Brace jiggled that crazy brow again, and she was tempted to ask about the scar—about the fine network of scars that snaked down the left side of his face. But she didn't. Oddly enough, she was more curious about the internal man than she was about external appearances. For instance, what made him so skittish? What made anyone in his right mind want to be a test pilot? And what on earth was a test pilot doing down here in a place like Coronoke? There weren't even any cars here, much less planes.

"Brace, how'd you get involved with—" she began, when he unfolded himself and stretched. Frances watched, fascinated, as flannel and denim moved smoothly over his lean, long torso, completely derailing her train of thought.

"Guess I'd better be going," he said, reaching for his flight jacket.

"But you—" She swallowed hard. "Yes, well... thanks again for all your many kindnesses these past two days. I can't imagine why you're being so nice to me when you obviously don't want me here, but I do appreciate it."

"I can't imagine, either. It's definitely not in character." He grinned, actuating a network of fine lines around his eyes. They really were remarkably nice eyes, she decided—clear, deep-set, rimmed with thick, stubby black lashes. Although the familiar message was back again. Keep out. No trespassing. Violators will be prosecuted to the full extent of the law.

Or towed at their own expense, she thought, amused. He had certainly tried hard enough.

But he needn't have worried. She was no threat to him or any other man, married, single or otherwise. As a three-time loser, whose father hadn't hung around much longer than it took to propagate—which made her a four-time loser, she supposed—Frances considered herself immunized for life.

Which made it all the more surprising that she wasn't ready to see him leave. She'd slept all day and wasn't sleepy yet, although she was certainly relaxed enough to sleep. They were both relaxed from all that high-octane, swamp gas bisque, but she had an idea sleep would be a long time coming.

The truth was she just didn't want to be alone. She wasn't used to being alone, no matter how she'd longed for a moment of solitude over the years. "I don't suppose you know anything about television sets, do you? All I've been able to get on Uncle Seymore's set is ghosts in a snowstorm."

"Sorry, mine's no better. Fringe area. No cable. If you've got a VCR, the Keegans have a pretty good library of videos. Books, too, if you need any reading material. Come by and help yourself, I never lock up unless I'm leaving the island."

"Thanks. Maybe I will in a day or so." He was getting ready to go, and she wanted to make him stay, and could have kicked herself for being so silly!

Pausing in the act of putting on his heavy flight jacket, Brace glanced over his shoulder, shadows emphasizing the irregularity of his features as well as those deep-set, enigmatic eyes. It occurred to Frances, that he had the look of a wounded warrior.

She realized that he also had the look of a man who could be lethal to any woman who was fool enough to fall in love with him.

He was moving toward the door, and she ached to beg him to stay just a little while longer. Because if he left, she might start thinking about all the bridges she'd burned behind her, and she didn't want to think about that now.

But she didn't beg, and he didn't offer. With every evidence of composure, she told him good night and watched until he disappeared down the narrow path under the low, overhanging branches. Gazing out into the darkness, she lingered in the open doorway until the quiet hum of the furnace reminded her that warm air was flowing out and cold air flowing in. Reluctantly she closed the door.

Funny... who would have thought the alien sound of water slapping against a shoreline could be so soothing to someone who'd grown up in a small inland town? Rivers didn't whisper to the shore, saying, "Shh...there now, there now, shh...."

At least the Maumee had never whispered to her.

Overhead, the sky was crisp and clear. Roughly a zillion stars shone brightly down, reflecting on the dark pewter surface of the Pamlico. Here there were no streetlights, no lighted windows up and down the block. No cheerful—or not so cheerful—household sounds. No lawn mowers, no blaring radios from passing cars, no dogs barking or children laughing in the yard next door.

Just "Shh, there now, there now, shh...."

Islands, she suspected, could be incredibly lonely places. One felt so vulnerable, surrounded by nothing but sky and water. Even Hatteras, the nearest land mass, was barely a mile wide, snaking out into the Atlantic some thirty-odd miles from the mainland.

Not for the first time, Frances wondered if she'd done the right thing by pulling up stakes and breaking all ties with her past.

Nearing the Hunt, his hands burrowed in his pockets, Brace savored the rich, iodiny smell of drying eelgrass. He'd done a lot of exploring when he'd first arrived. Being alone at night on a small island invited introspection, and once the Keegans left, he'd walked relentlessly, day and night, slogging through knee-deep marsh, hacking his way through a jungle of scrubby trees, palmetto and ropelike vines, until he was tired enough to sleep without dreaming.

Only gradually had he realized that thinking about the past—about Sharon, and about his own mortality—was beginning to lose its power over him. For years he'd been running, but there came a time when a man had to either accept what he'd made of his life, change it or check out. Of all the many things he'd been called over the years, no one had ever called him a quitter.

Tonight, however, it wasn't Brace Ridgeway, street kid, jailbird, daredevil and all around hardcase he was thinking about. Against his better judgment, his thoughts kept drifting back to Frances Jones of the lavender blue eyes and the parchment-pale skin, the long, elegant bones and the glossy hair that slithered like strands of liquid black glass when she turned her head suddenly.

Who the hell was she? What was she doing alone in a place like this? At a time like this? It didn't add up.

She was an intelligent woman, even a beautiful one in her own way—a way he was just now coming to appreciate. Brace's taste in women had always run to something a little flashier. The plain truth was, he liked a dash of slut in his women—maybe because he felt comfortable with it. Society broads with their finishing school accents and their elitist pretensions gave him a royal bellyache. He'd tangled with a few of that particular breed in his formative years, in the process of being bounced from one agency to another, one foster home to another. A few more when he was older, when he discovered that some of them enjoyed the occasional night of slumming.

For a long time Brace had prided himself on being tough, but after a couple of decades, toughness got to be more trouble than it was worth. Somewhere along the way he'd learned that lurking underneath his hard shell were a few spooky shadows and some crater-size hollows. He'd managed to light up most of the shadows, but when he'd tried to fill in one of the hollows with a woman named Sharon Bing, the whole thing had blown up in his face.

Life's lesson number 629. Don't invest more than you can afford to lose. In anything. Especially a woman.

Frances Jones—Frances *Smith* Jones, as she'd taken care to point out after her second bowl of his soup—was a slightly different species. He hadn't gotten her pegged quite yet. She'd been married. There was a distinct mark on her third finger, left hand, where a ring had recently been removed. The thing that didn't compute was why a woman of her type would come to a place like Coronoke in the dead of winter, alone. She didn't strike him as the quitting type. On the other hand, she was here. And she was definitely alone.

Whatever had happened to her marriage had nothing to do with him. All the same, he couldn't help being mildly curious . . . in a purely impersonal way.

Brace had never considered himself a cynic. He was simply a realist. Even so, he'd have thought a woman like Frances Smith Jones would've hung in there, even when the going got tough. Pride, for one thing. She had it in spades.

He grinned, remembering the way she'd gone toe-to-toe with him those first few days. If it hadn't been for that flu bug that had laid her out, she'd still have been in there slugging.

So he wondered about her. Idly standing at the water's edge out behind the Hunt, he gazed out over the Pamlico toward Hatteras Inlet, toward Ocracoke Island, and wondered about a lot of things, such as what her husband was like and why they'd split and what she was doing so far off the beaten track. Hell, Coronoke wasn't even on most maps!

Not that it mattered one way or another to him. He happened to have an inquiring mind, and there wasn't a whole lot to distract him. Besides which, he'd been left in charge of things around here when the Keegans had headed west, which meant that, whether he liked it or not, she was one more responsibility. So maybe he'd just look in on her from time to time, just to be sure she was okay. No big deal.

Back at Blackbeard's Hole, Frances slathered moisturizer on her face and then leaned closer to frown into the mirror. Was that a wrinkle starting between her eyebrows or just a shadow?

It was a wrinkle. Oh, for pity's sake, she was falling apart! In another few months she'd be forty years old.

Who was it who said that life began at forty? Ten bucks said it hadn't been a woman.

"Look on the bright side, pal." She flashed her teeth in a clench-jawed grimace. Forty with a published book to her credit and a résumé that included one hospital, two nursing homes and a couple of monthly columns—forty with no debts, no dependents and no strings attached....

That kind of forty, even with a wrinkle or two, was a whale of a lot better than thirty with a two-timing husband, a pair of parasitic in-laws, a younger sister needing braces, twin brothers in college and a job that was in danger of being terminated. She'd had all that on her plate ten years ago and managed to survive.

The grimace segued into a genuine smile. She was okay. She was pretty damned good, in fact! She still had her family, no matter how scattered they were. And she had herself.

First thing in the morning, Frances vowed, she was going to proof her last column and get it in the mail, and then she was going to tackle that manuscript. It was all but finished, lacking only the final polish, plus maybe a few more additions in the snacks section. Low-fat snacks were easy. *Good,* nutritious low-fat snacks were a little harder to come by, but she'd brought along her notes. All she needed were a few additions to the snacks chapter.

Brace's Best Bourbon Brisk? Aside from the fact that soup could hardly be considered a snack, it would no more fit into her cookbook than the man himself would fit into her new life.

The trouble was he was already a part of her new life. Strictly a temporary part, but all the same...

All the same, nothing! He'd caught her at a bad moment, when neither of them had had much choice. But now that she was on her feet again, things were going to be different. She would simply be too busy to see him, and after a while, he'd get the message.

Frances's remaining ability to trust had gone down the drain when she'd learned that her dear, departed husband had kept a mistress for nine of the eleven years they'd been married. Not only that, but his family—that pair of sweet, soft-spoken leeches who'd moved in with them six months after she and Ken had bought the modest house on Elm Street and stayed on even after Ken had died—had known about the other woman almost from the first.

All those years she'd been sharing her husband with her own hairdresser, for pity's sake! The woman who had practically scalped her and then told her her neck was too long to wear her hair short. The woman who had pointed out every new line and wrinkle and gray hair the minute it had appeared!

She'd been a blind fool, a gullible wimp, a doormat. Well, no more! *This* Frances Smith Jones—and that, too, was going to change! From this moment on, she was plain Frances Smith. And plain Frances Smith was a lot tougher than she looked!

A *test* pilot, for heaven's sake!

Five

The cheese spread made with fat-free cottage cheese and reduced-fat cheddar was not half-bad, Frances decided. It was a good source of calcium and protein. Actually, it tasted good, too—especially served on a cheese-flavored rice cake. Although, perhaps a spoonful of low-fat mayonnaise...or maybe a dash of Tabasco?

"Tabasco! Oh, for pity's sake!"

She chewed on her pencil, made a few notations in her recipe book and chewed on her pencil some more.

A *test* pilot, for crying out loud! A man who put hot sauce in his tomato soup. A tough, couthless creature who, at the drop of a hat, swore like a sailor's parrot.

Her father had been a scientist. All five feet five inches, one hundred twenty-seven pounds of him. The harshest thing she ever remembered hearing him utter during one of his rare visits home, was "Saints alive, Frances, can't you keep them quiet?"

Ken, too, had been a model of rectitude. A handsome, well-dressed, civic-minded insurance salesman, he had even gone to PTA meetings, despite the fact that he'd never wanted children. Frances, who had wanted children, had found it ironic that her friend, Allie Schultz, who had three boys, had claimed it would take an act of congress to get her husband to a PTA meeting—or any meeting other than his bowling league.

Ken had said he went only because his firm insured the school's athletic department. Florence and Henry, she recalled now, had both smirked. Frances often thought that if they could have figured out a way to do it, they would have bronzed every syllable that fell from their only son's thin, lying lips. Invariably she'd felt guilty after any such ungenerous thought. It was only natural for parents to be proud of their offspring, even when he was a philandering jerk!

She wouldn't have felt quite so guilty had she known that the female barracuda who butchered her hair had a son in that particular school, a child who might or might not have been Ken's son. That fact, along with everything else, had come out when she'd found that indiscreet note from "Kiki" in an old briefcase two years after Ken's death. Addressed to Ken at his office, the mushy, untidily scribbled epistle had been shockingly explicit about both the nature and the duration of their relationship.

Florence and Henry had tried to bluff it out at first, pretending that their poor, dear Kenny had only been showing a simple friendly interest in the family hairdresser and her poor, fatherless child. Unfortunately the whole town had been in on it. Once the dam had sprung the first leak, Frances had been treated to all the gossip she'd been shielded from over the years through a combination of good intentions and her own blind gullibility.

"Friendly interest, my left hind leg!" she snorted, slamming down her spiral notebook filled with ideas for new recipes she'd accumulated over the years.

Slathering a thick layer of the low-fat pimento cheese substitute onto a cheddar-flavored rice cake, she bit into it viciously. Even her closest friends had been in on the conspiracy! Allie, who handled classifieds at the magazine, had explained that everyone thought Frances knew but had too much pride to acknowledge it, which was why no one dared mention it in her hearing.

Pride! As if any woman with a grain of genuine pride would put up with a lying, two-timing, no-good weasel!

Three days after she'd found the letter, she'd made up her mind, but it had taken more than a week to complete all the arrangements. Her immediate impulse had been to turn the Smiths out into the street and let them find someone else to sponge off.

Unfortunately she knew herself well enough to know that her conscience would get in the way. Instead, she'd signed the house over to them, figuring whatever equity she had accumulated would be more than enough to assuage any twinges of conscience.

It wasn't as if they'd been penniless. Ken had never gotten around to changing the beneficiary of his term life policy from his parents to his wife. A rather glaring oversight for an insurance salesman, she'd thought at the time.

Two years later she had wondered fleetingly if he'd had yet another policy made out in favor of his little hairdresser, but by then she'd no longer cared. All she'd wanted was to walk away from everything he had ever touched, turning her back on a legacy of bitterness, hollow memories and shattered illusions.

And dammit, she refused to allow them to follow her to Coronoke!

Making up her mind suddenly, Frances spooned some of the ersatz pimento cheese spread—Fancy's Funky Faux Cheese Spread?—into a plastic container, grabbed a roll of rice cakes and headed out the door. There were times when even lousy company was better than no company at all.

Not that Brace was lousy company. At least not since he'd made up his mind she wasn't a fugitive from the law, hiding out on his precious island. He didn't trust her? Fine. She didn't trust him, either. But that didn't mean they couldn't behave like reasonable adults.

He was chopping wood. Following the sounds, she found him on the far side of the magnificent, sprawling ruin called the Hunt. Despite the forty-five-degree temperature, his shirt had been tossed over the silvered branch of a dead cedar tree. His jeans rode dangerously low on his narrow hips and crumpled over the tops of his heavy work boots as he swung the ax over his head.

Clutching the cheese and rice cakes to her bosom, Frances ogled at the flexing of all those muscles. Skinny? No way! Lean he might be, but there was no way all that sinewy, sweat-polished masculinity could ever be called skinny!

The damp hair on his chest looked black. The hair on his head, thick and shaggy, with more than a hint of gray, was a dozen shades of brown.

Ken's body had been smooth, the hair on his head, blond and impeccably groomed. Thanks to frequent trips to his favorite hairdresser.

Dismissing all thought of her late husband, Frances wondered absently why the sight of coarse, curly hair on a man's body should have such a remarkable effect on her involuntary reflexes.

The ax flashed down, neatly splitting a chunk of wood into two halves, and as if he'd known of her presence all along, he buried the blade in the scarred stump, brushed his hands on the seat of his pants and turned to her with a coolly evaluating look. "What can I do for you?"

It would never occur to the man that she might merely want his company, she thought, irritated for no real reason. "Here, try this. It's a spread—or maybe a dip. Put it on one of these things and then tell me honestly what you think." She shoved the plastic container and the roll of rice cakes at him, leaving him no choice but to take them from her.

"Do I use my pocket knife, my fingers, or will the ax do?"

"Sorry. It was just an impulse. I'm not very good at it yet."

"Not very good at what?" He was watching her as if he half suspected her of trying to poison him.

For pity's sake, she thought, she'd eaten *his* food without hesitation. The least he could do was return the courtesy! Her shoulders slumped in discouragement. It had been a lousy idea. She was good at lousy ideas.

"Not very good at what?" he repeated, lifting his split-level eyebrow imperceptibly.

"Acting impulsively. I think maybe you have to be born with the gene. I should've brought a knife."

He grinned, rearranging an oddly attractive assortment of mismatched features. "Perish the thought," he drawled, a glint of humor showing in his cool gray eyes. Hooking his shirt with one finger, he nodded toward the house, and after only a moment's hesitation, Frances followed him inside. While he washed up at the kitchen sink, Frances watched, amused at the thought that poor Florence would've expired on the spot if either Ken or Henry had done anything so uncouth.

While he dried his face and hands on the kitchen towel, she spread a rice cake with the experimental cheese mixture, placed it on a saucer and then crossed her arms over her chest, as if daring him to sample it.

"I really do need a second opinion. My taste buds haven't quite recovered from the flu, so be honest with me now. It's for my book."

He looked at the cheese-spread rice cake, then looked at her, his gaze moving deliberately from her windblown hair to her pink turtleneck shirt to her jeans, which had been chosen for comfort and not for style...unfortunately. "Should I have an antidote handy before I taste it?"

Naked from the waist up, except for the towel which he'd slung around his neck, he dragged a chair out, straddled it and picked up the rice cake.

"Would I poison you? Brace, I owe you—remember?"

"Don't forget, I tried to run you off."

"And then you nursed me through the flu. So we're even."

He shot her a skeptical look and cautiously took a small bite. Frances waited, her eyes lingering on his mouth. He had beautiful teeth. She'd almost forgotten that she'd once thought of him as old Flint-Face. Actually, his face was more like polished oak.

Pity. Flint-Face had more of a ring to it than Oak-Face. "Well?"

"You want my unbiased opinion?"

She grimaced. "When you put it that way, I'm not so sure." She'd wanted him to rave. She'd wanted him to tell her she was a creative genius.

No, that wasn't what she'd wanted. What she'd *really* wanted was so absurd it was embarrassing. "I never claimed it was real pimento cheese. It's a fat-free, low sodium substitute. So... what do you think? Is it any good?" She waited, admiring the hand that held the half-eaten rice cake. It was a man's hand. There was nothing at all smooth or delicate about it.

He took another bite, and Frances watched his throat, fascinated by the subtle play of muscles under his smooth, tanned skin. She told herself it didn't matter whether or not he approved, but it did, so she waited some more.

He was doing it to her deliberately. She crossed her arms over her A-cups and began to tap her foot on the gritty floor, her limited supply of patience rapidly running out.

"Tabasco," he pronounced finally.

"What?" she squawked.

"I said—"

"I heard what you said! Is that the only seasoning you know? What is it with test pilots—do you all have asbestos-lined gullets?"

He shrugged. "You said you needed an unbiased opinion. That's what you got."

Heaving a vast sigh, she dropped into a kitchen chair and plopped her chin down on her fist. "What I need is a guinea pig whose taste buds haven't already been cauterized. I'm half a chapter short of finishing, and the blasted manuscript was due in New York on the fifteenth, so what happens? First I lose my printer and now the only test taster for miles around makes a habit of pigging out on hot sauce."

"I see," Brace said, not seeing at all. The woman was a writer, working on a cookbook. Which probably accounted for the laptop, the box of cooking equipment and all those five-pound sacks of whole-grain this and that. Not your typical vacation fare.

But just where he was supposed to fit in was another story. The score was even, she'd said, and he'd just as soon keep it that way. After a few subtle whiffs of her spicy, grassy scent—after undressing her from the skin out and changing her nightgown twice while she was too sick to protest—after watching those crushed-violet eyes of hers go from shadows to sunlight and back again, his internal alarm system was already pegging well into the red. Every instinct he possessed was screaming, "Back off, lady!"

He sighed. "Look, maybe if I try another one—" He was reaching for the container when the phone rang. Relieved at the unexpected reprieve, he practically tripped over his chair trying to get to it. "Sorry," he said with a glance over his shoulder. "Maybe another time, okay?"

Oh, certainly. Like the thirty-first of February. Frances could practically hear the words.

Scowling at the bright yellow plastic container, she tried hard to hide her disappointment. Really, she was being more than a little childish! Perhaps he was right, and a drop or two of hot sauce would perk it up. It was worth a try. She could list it among the optional ingredients, along with the chopped cilantro. Unlike her other two optionals, green olives and sunflower seeds, hot sauce would hardly increase the fat content.

Ignoring the low-pitched conversation going on across the room, she rinsed off the knife and put the lid on the container. One basic recipe with enough variations just might be enough to finish out the snacks section. Served on celery, served on rice cakes, served on—

And what about chutney? Served on a whole wheat wafer with—

"No, dammit, you can't come down here! I said—"

On the point of easing out the door, Frances hesitated. She wasn't eavesdropping, but with the man practically yelling in her ear, not ten feet away from where she stood, there was no way she could avoid overhearing his end of the conversation.

"Listen, I've told you I'm not ready yet! When I make up my mind, you'll be the first to know, but dammit, Sharon, you keep bugging me this way and we'll call it off right now!"

Call what off? Sharon who?

"Yeah, yeah—listen, will you just put Pete on the line?"

Frances closed the door quietly behind her.

Two days passed before she saw him again. The first day, she finished proofing her column and got it ready to mail. The next morning, without asking permission, she checked out one of the smaller boats, the same one he had used to rescue her the day after she'd arrived. This time she looked to be sure there was enough fuel in the container to get her to the marina and back. Some lessons a woman learned the first time around.

And others, she didn't.

Brace was waiting on the dock when she made her triumphant return. Triumphant because she didn't bump a single piling, and because she'd mailed in her final column, located someone who would print up her manuscript when she was finished with it and made a successful raid on the Red and White. She'd made a rather inelegant approach to the marina dock after the trip over to Hatteras, and Jerry had offered her some pointers, which helped enormously. In return, she'd promised him some of her fat-free, low-sugar, but perfectly delectable apple coffee cake the next time she baked.

Brace looked even more grim than he'd looked the first time he'd met her at the dock. He stood and reached for the groceries, and she handed them up. Neither of them spoke. They might as well have been on two separate islands.

Was it something she'd said? Something she hadn't said? Should she have asked his permission to take the boat?

Oh, for pity's sake, this was downright childish!

He set the sacks aside and reached down a hand to help her up onto the pier, and after only the briefest hesitation, she took it. His palm was hard and dry, and Frances told herself there was no reason in the world why she should feel the shock waves right down to her knees. She must've imagined it.

"I got some Tabasco," she ventured, unobtrusively rubbing her palm on the leg of her baggy flannels.

His ice gray eyes began to thaw, and after a moment, he almost smiled. "Smart move. Catsup and Tabasco cover a multitude of sins."

Speaking of sins, it occurred to Frances that the Mona Lisa had nothing on Brace Ridgeway. That quirky little half smile of his was downright wicked. He was a bundle of contradictions, and he was beginning to interest her a little too much. If she still had a grain of all that common sense she was reputed to possess, she'd have left the minute he'd marched down to the shore to warn her off.

Deliberately she gathered up two sacks of groceries and set out toward the path. If he brought the third one, fine. If he didn't, she'd come back for it. The way to avoid disappointment, she reminded herself, was to lower her expectations. One more lesson learned the hard way.

He was right behind her. "Like I said, a dash of catsup and Tabasco can cover up the worst mistakes. Me, I'm not much of a cook."

"Me, I am," she said dryly. "In fact, cooking is my stock in trade."

"Is that supposed to be a pun?"

"I'm a better cook than I am a comedian."

"God, I hope so!"

By the end of the week, they had settled into a comfortable, if wary, truce. Using Brace as her guinea pig, Frances ran one last test of all the recipes in the final chapter, and a few she simply thought he might enjoy. He didn't need to know they'd been thoroughly tested before.

She took him a batch of her basic low-fat granola, made with raw oatmeal, wheat germ, raisins and sunflower seeds, divided into serving-sized portions with a different blend of spices in each serving. The plastic bags were numbered, some with sweetner, some without, and he dutifully reported on his favorites.

Toward the end of the second week, they drifted cautiously into sharing lunch and dinner, as well. Brace provided the raw materials, Frances cooked, and neither of them had very much to say. Brace usually left soon after the meal, and she told herself she was glad, because if he'd stayed—if they'd begun to drift into even a slightly warmer relationship, she might have forgotten all the reasons she had for not trusting any man ever again.

The trouble was that he got to her without even trying. The man was too thin! He reminded her of a starving wolf, too wild to accept help, but too hungry not to be tempted. To make matters worse, she was beginning to suspect that food was not all he was starved for.

And as soon as she started feeling that way, she reminded herself forcefully of Adam Westphall, who had taken her heart and her virginity, but graciously declined to accept her family—and of Paul Capro, who had courted her, dumped her, impregnated her best friend and then left town forever.

She reminded herself of her own father, who had managed to sire a flock of children before disappearing into the Brazilian rain forest, leaving them to get along as best they could.

And of sweet, gentle, kind-to-his-parents Kenneth Randolph Jones, with his flawlessly manicured fingernails, his flawlessly groomed hair, his old-fashioned manners and the morals of a tomcat.

So maybe Brace Ridgeway was too thin. Maybe now and then she caught a look in his eyes that reminded her of a homeless stray who'd all but forgotten what it was like to be warm, safe and well fed.

So maybe she'd feed him. She might even go the extra mile and cook up some rich dishes designed to put a few pounds on his lanky frame, but that was *all* she would do. She was no bleeding heart, out to rescue society's rejects. She was merely a dietitian, a nutritionist, a food columnist and the author of—with a little luck and a lot of hard work—a soon-to-be-published cookbook.

Besides, if he wanted company, he could invite "Sharon" down to visit. From the sound of it, they weren't exactly strangers.

She bought salty, sugar-cured, hickory-smoked bacon. She bought real butter, not the fake stuff. She bought tenderloin of beef with no thought to the cholesterol and made potatoes au gratin with aged New York cheddar. She baked a batch of her little raisin-cheese tarts using four percent cottage cheese and real eggs instead of cholesterol-free substitutes, and fried chicken the way her aunt Rowena from Georgia used to fry it, in bacon drippings. To assuage her conscience, she made a big batch of brown rice and black beans with chopped raw onion, parsley, cumin and lemon juice.

In return, Brace brought her gray trout and an enormous rib roast. He kept her boat running, refilled the fuel tank, repaired a shutter that had pulled loose and a commode tank that wouldn't stop running—both of which repairs she could have made herself, but it was nice not to have to.

"Lady, you can evermore cook," he said now with a sigh as he leaned back in her uncle's big lounge chair and closed his eyes. She had fed him a full four course meal, without substituting low-fat options. He had probably ingested three days' worth of calories in one sitting, and she didn't even want to think about the saturated fat. At least he ate all his broccoli and sweet potato.

Then, too, he was a big man. As her eyes strayed over his relaxed form, Frances was reminded of just how very big he was. Kenneth had been exactly her height. Paul and Adam had been a bit taller, but slender. Even at his thinnest, Brace Ridgeway could never be called slender. Rangy, maybe. Even gaunt. Lean and mean would be a more apt description... although his disposition seemed to be improving lately. He hadn't snarled at her in almost three days. Hadn't even scowled at her in two.

"Why'd you split up?" he asked without opening his eyes.

Frances, nursing her cappuccino, did a double take. "I beg your pardon? Split what up?"

"You were married, right? You're here alone. So why'd you dump him?"

"Not that it's any of your business, but my husband died in an automobile accident two years ago."

Brace swore quietly. "Judas priest. I'm sorry, Fancy, I had no business saying a damn fool thing like that."

"No, you didn't." But since he had, she felt free to return the favor. "What happened to your face?"

He didn't move, not so much as the flicker of an eyelash, but suddenly the atmosphere crackled with tension. "What makes you think something did? Maybe I was just born ugly."

He was far from ugly, and she suspected he knew it. "I recognize plastic surgery when I see it. My youngest brother skateboarded through a plate glass door when he was fourteen. They did a better job on your nose than they did on his. Does it work right?"

Brace fingered the slope of his reconstructed nose. "Yeah, I guess. By the time I took that last dive, it had already been broken three times. Is there any of that pie left?"

"Practically all of it."

"Well, what about it? Do I have to beg?"

"At a guess, I'd say you've never begged in your life."

"Don't be too sure of that," he said with a dry bitterness that belied his lazy drawl. He was watching her through slitted eyes, and Frances wondered what he thought of what he saw. Suddenly she wished she'd put on more than moisturizer and a slash of lipstick. Wished she were younger, more attractive—less terrified of being hurt again.

"I don't suppose you have trouble with blood sugar," she teased. "That pie's loaded."

He came out of the lounge chair in one smooth motion. "Forget it," he snarled as he snatched up his battered leather flight jacket.

While Frances watched, wondering what had set him off, he slammed out into the clear, cold night, leaving her angry, confused, and feeling as if she'd let something valuable slip from her grasp.

For a long time Brace stood on the end of the pier, staring out over the Pamlico Sound. Now and then he caught a flash of fluorescence in the depths of the still, dark water as something swam past.

She probably thought he'd lost his mind. Maybe he had. Otherwise he'd have known better than to try and get too close.

Cold, damp night air fingered in through the open front of his coat, chilling his overheated flesh, and deliberately Brace forced himself to think about Sharon—to visualize the picture he'd kept close by until a few weeks ago. It was presently underneath the Keegans' heavy bookcase where it had slid when he'd slung his coat across a table and knocked it to the floor. He hadn't bothered to rake it out.

But maybe he'd better retrieve the thing, if only to remind him of what could happen when a guy let down his guard too far. When the weather turned cold and the nights were long and empty, it was tempting to hunt for warmth and companionship. But warmth and companionship could be a double-edged sword. Solo wasn't a bad way to go. He was used to it. At least when he got burned, he knew where to place the blame.

The firing began just before daybreak. Frances bolted up out of a dream of hundreds of birthday cakes all lined up with candles ablaze, like a Fourth of July fireworks display.

"I wish the damned ducks would shoot back," she muttered, and tried covering her head with the pillow. It didn't work, and after a while she got up and dressed. Over coffee she worked on finishing up the index.

The firing went on sporadically all day as the weather grew increasingly rough. By noon, dark clouds had moved in from the west to cover more than half the

sky. Frances cooked lemon-chicken soup for lunch and
made crisp bread. Brace never showed up.

By evening a blowing rain had commenced. For
dinner she broiled the fish he had brought the day before and made parsley potatoes and braised French-cut
green beans. She ate alone by candlelight.

She was reading the same page over for the third time
when someone pounded on her front door. By then the
wind was howling like a pack of wolves, driving rain in
horizontal sheets against the windows.

It would serve him right if she let him stay out there
until his joints rusted, but with her heart turning cart-
wheels she flung aside her book and hurried to let him
in. Holding the door against the wind, she squinted
into the darkness and tried to control her smile. "For
pity's sake, Brace, what are you doing out in all
this—"

The smile faded. Her voice broke off as she stared at
the three red-faced strangers, two dressed in camou-
flage and one in hunting orange. They leaned toward
her and she fell back, recoiling from the whiskey
fumes. A moment too late she shoved back, at the same
time trying to slam the door shut, but she was no match
for roughly five hundred pounds of combined weight.

They didn't even have to push. All they had to do
was lean. She fell back and the hunters fell inside, and
suddenly she was very frightened.

Gathering her courage, she tried to sound authori-
tative. "The house you're looking for is farther along
the path."

They wouldn't have recognized authority if it wore
five stars and a badge. "Hey, lookee here what I
found," crowed the youngest of the trio. He was about

a hundred pounds overweight and cheerfully, obnoxiously, soused to the gills.

"Jus' wanna come in outta the rain, l'il sugar," said the one in the orange vest. He lurched, tripped on a rug, and Frances dodged behind a chair.

"Look, I'm afraid you've made a mistake. This is not the lodge. The man you're looking for is—"

"Not lookin' for a man, sweetcakes. Reck'n we already found what we're lookin' for, ain't that right, Charlie?" This one had curly, black hair under a sweat-stained orange cap, and the kind of overblown good looks that appealed to some women, but not to Frances. Not in a million years.

She eyed the bedroom door, trying frantically to remember whether there was a latch on the inside. If only she were closer to the back door! If only—

Curly-Hair lunged again, catching her by the shoulder. He kicked the chair aside and tugged her against his padded chest, and Frances, off-balance, twisted her face aside. He smelled like a distillery. They all did. "I'm warning you, if you don't—"

"Hey, look at this, guys—pie!" The fat one dug out three fingerfuls of filling and shoved it toward his mouth, dripping some on the floor and the rest down the front of his canvas coat. "Hey, this's damn fine stuff!"

"So's this," Curly crowed, dragging her back into his arms when she would have escaped. She kicked at his booted foot and bit her lip as pain throbbed through her bruised bare toe. If she could just get her knee free—

"Looks like you boys wandered off course" came a silky drawl from the doorway. The fat one, who had just uncorked her bottle of Madeira, dropped it on the counter, where it rolled off onto the floor, emptying the sticky contents down the front of the cabinet and across the gleaming white vinyl. Pie-Face glanced over his shoulder, spilling another fistful of lemon-curd filling into the mess. Curly clamped her around the neck with one arm and fumbled under his coat with his other hand, and while he was distracted, Frances jabbed him in the side with her elbow.

It was all the opening Brace needed. Suddenly two of the men were out on the deck, facedown. The one who still held Frances hostage was blubbering something about no harm intended while he tried to untangle a handgun from a holster that had caught in the game flap of his hunting coat.

Then, he, too was on the floor, with one arm twisted up behind him. Brace, kneeling over him, glanced up. "You all right, Fancy?"

"F-f-f— Yes," she whispered.

"I'll put out the garbage and be right back, don't lock up yet."

Lock up? From now on she would not only lock up, she would shove the biggest piece of furniture in the house under the doorknob! She would nail the doors and windows shut, she would—

"No, I won't," she managed as Brace frog marched the curly-haired lothario out into the cold, blowing rain.

"If you've sobered up by then, you can come back and collect your hardware tomorrow," she heard him say as he gathered up an armload of high-powered armament from beside the front door. "But if you're not off this island in five minutes flat, don't even bother to come back. There won't be enough left to make the trip worth your time."

"Hey, that's a twelve-hundred-dollar shotgun, man!"

"Four minutes and counting."

"Come on, man, we didn't mean no harm, we were only—"

Brace broke one of the shotguns, checked both chambers and then lifted it to his shoulder, sighting along one of the twin barrels. The sounds of cursing quickly faded away, to be replaced by the peaceful drone of rain and the howl of a northeast wind.

Shivering, Frances wrapped her arms around her body to keep from falling apart while she waited for him to come back inside. Funny, she thought—independence no longer seemed quite so desirable. Crazy or not, all in the world she wanted at this moment was a pair of strong male arms to hold her until she could stop shaking. The thought that it had been another pair of strong male arms that had started her to shaking in the first place never entered her mind.

This was Brace. And while they might not be exactly friends, she trusted him. Against all reason, against everything she had learned over a long and lusterless lifetime, she had somehow come to trust him in a way she had never before trusted anyone.

Six

"They won't bother you again," said Brace. Scowling, he closed the door behind him. "They hadn't bagged their limit. The longer it took, the more they drank. Those old blinds don't offer much protection from the weather, so when the rain set in, they saw your light and decided to come calling."

"I'm amazed they could even walk that far." Except for an occasional tremor, Frances was no longer shaking.

Brace took in her pallor and the unnatural brightness of her eyes. With her arms wrapped tightly around her chest, she looked frightened, defensive and altogether too vulnerable.

"I don't suppose you have any brandy?"

"No, and don't offer me any of your bourbon. I'll just put on a robe and nudge the thermostat."

"Keegan's bourbon, not mine. What about that sweet stuff you flavored the apples with the other night?"

"It was Madeira but I don't need it. I don't need spirits, I don't need baby-sitting and I certainly don't need—" She broke off at the sound of a sharp report just outside the window. "Oh, God," she whispered, "they're back!"

"Tree branch snapped off. Look, sit down before you collapse. If you'll tell me where your bathrobe is, I'll get it for you." His voice was terse, his manner brisk as he filled the kettle and put it on to heat.

Not for a ten-pound box of Godiva chocolates would she have admitted it, but Frances was just as glad he hadn't taken her at her word. She *wasn't* fine. She didn't want to be alone right now. Alone in a familiar house on a familiar street in a familiar neighborhood was one thing. Alone in a strange cottage on a deserted island where the closest thing to civilization was a boat ride away was quite another.

"I see you finally located your uncle's stash of blankets," Brace said as he emerged from the bedroom. He held the flannel bathrobe while she shoved her arms in the sleeves, then he lifted her bare feet onto the hassock and tucked a cotton blanket around her legs.

"Top closet shelf. I stood on a chair. I'm using all three, and it's barely enough."

"Enough for the occasional cool summer night. Not many calls for winter rentals, according to Keegan. It would mean turning on the water and then draining the system again. Incidentally, how'd you manage that first night?"

She sent him a wry look. "Common sense and a basic knowledge of plumbing," she said as he tossed a double handful of tea leaves into the kettle of boiling water and sat it back on the burner. Frances liked her tea strong, but not caustic. "Milk in mine, please. Lots of milk."

They sipped the powerful brew and listened to the keening wind. Frances wrapped her icy fingers around the mug and savored the warmth. Brace straddled a straight chair and gulped his own black tea as if it were water.

"You should've added milk. Undiluted tannic acid's not good for the human digestive system," she said. "Sorry. Another habit."

"Anybody ever call you a busybody?"

"Everybody." Frances knew by the wicked gleam in his eye that he was teasing. There was no way she could take offense. As the warmth gradually took effect, the tension that had gripped her ever since she had opened her door to three armed, inebriated strangers began to dissolve. "Brace, I owe you another batch of thanks. If you hadn't come along..."

"I reckon you could've handled it," he said casually. He reckoned no such thing. Thank God he'd been too restless to sleep. Guns and alcohol were a lethal combination.

Frances stared down at her empty mug. "Once, years ago," she said, her voice unnaturally calm, "a neighbor's boy cut the screen on my back door and came in while I was in the shower. Before I even knew he was in the house, he'd helped himself to sixteen dollars I'd left on the hall table to pay the dry cleaner. I caught him on the way out, and it never occurred to me to be frightened—at least, not much—because I knew him. But these men—they were strangers! They were drinking and they had guns, and I..." She shuddered. Her eyes were suddenly too bright.

Brace didn't like that glittery look. He'd seen it before after someone had had a close call. A stiff drink might've helped. A good night's sleep would probably do the trick. But right now she needed a friend here with her. She didn't need to be alone.

The trouble was, he was all she had.

Setting his empty mug on the floor, he moved closer and gathered up her legs. The hassock was old, lopsided and too low for any guy who had to jackknife himself into a standard cockpit.

In spite of that, he perched there and began massaging her blanket-covered feet. Taking care of this irritatingly independent woman was getting to be a habit. "Shh, don't sweat it, Jonesie."

"I've d-d-decided to drop the Jones. But you can call me Smitty if you want to." She finished off her tea with a shuddering grimace and held out her mug.

"More?"

"Heaven forfend. However, I'm sure it was just what I needed."

"Yeah, right."

For some reason Frances couldn't seem to tear her gaze from his face as he massaged her icy feet with his big, hard hands. When he smiled, which was practically never, his face took on an altogether different attitude. It was almost as if she could see another person peering out from behind that tough, patchwork mask.

Which was an indication of just how shaken she was. Never had anyone ever accused her of being fanciful. Even her most creative recipes had evolved, for the most part, from old standbys, one cautious step at a time.

All the same there was definitely more to Brace Ridgeway than a surly disposition and a philistine's palate. At the moment just having him nearby gave her a warm, secure feeling.

Which in turn gave her a distinctly uneasy feeling!

Reluctantly she shifted her legs off his lap and immediately missed the comforting weight of his hands on her feet.

How disconcerting! It had been so long since any man had touched her—so long since she'd even wanted a man's touch—that she forced a bright smile and blurted out the first thing that popped into her mind.

"I wonder if it takes a lawyer to resume a maiden name."

"Never having had a maiden name, I wouldn't presume to advise you. Smitty, hmm? I think I prefer Fancy."

"It doesn't fit. I only used it for publication."

"What's wrong with Jones?"

"It belonged to my husband." Which told him something about her marriage. "Since he's not here to object, I don't see why I can't just declare myself a Smith again and send out those little cards you get from the post office when you move—only names, not addresses."

"No kids, I take it?"

She nibbled her bottom lip, and Brace found his attention distracted. Absently he resumed stroking the soles of her feet, and with an almost infinitesimal sigh, she said, "No kids."

He found her toes through the blanket and began to explore each one in turn. "Any particular reason?"

With his wonderful hands doing wonderful things to her cold feet, Frances would've told him anything he asked, up to and including her age. "Not really. I wanted one. Actually, I wanted half a dozen, but it just didn't happen."

"Any particular reason?" Brace repeated. *Back off, man! That's strictly need-to-know stuff, and you don't!*

She shrugged and the cotton blanket slipped from her shoulders, baring an elegant neck that looked almost too delicate to bear the weight of all that dark, slithery hair. Some of the color had returned to her face, and Brace found himself admiring the delicate flush of pink-stained ivory surrounded by red flannel.

"Timing, I guess," she said with a sad little smile that ripped right through his gut. "I was working two jobs for a while—we'd just bought a house—and then Ken's parents moved in with us, and they required a lot of attention. Ken kept wanting to build up a nest egg before we started a family, but even on two salaries, we barely kept afloat."

"Tough."

Bruised-violet eyes took on a fleeting look of bitterness, which caused him to wonder, but then she yawned. "Not really. Look, I didn't mean to be so much trouble. I'm beginning to understand why you don't want me here, though. The funny thing is, I've always been perfectly self-sufficient. I was always the one other people came to when they needed a hand, and now, here I am—draped around your neck like an albatross."

"No problem," he said.

Big problem, he thought. He was just beginning to suspect how big a problem it was.

"How about if I bake you a lemon-poppy-seed cake tomorrow and then stay out of your hair completely?

Until the end of time?'' She quirked a funny little grin.
"Or at least until I get this blasted manuscript printed
up and in the mail and then figure out what I'm going
to do with the rest of my life. Is it a deal?''

It was a deal, but it was a lousy deal, Brace told
himself three days later. The hunters had come back
long enough to collect their firearms. Brace had not
encouraged them to return. He'd checked out the three
crude board-and-brush duck blinds that had been in
general use by nonresidents for years. According to
Keegan, Hurricane Emily had dismantled a couple.
Hurricane season was over, but Maudie had warned
him that the hard nor'easters that ripped the coast between October and March could be even more dangerous. Maybe the next one would polish off those last
three duck blinds.

Frances brought over the cake and a pot of vegetar-
ian chili that wasn't half-bad with the addition of a
generous shot of Texas Pete. After that she disappeared. Brace told himself he was glad, that her absence was precisely what he'd been trying so damned
hard to achieve. The trouble was he couldn't convince
himself. Just knowing she was there, only a few hundred yards away, was getting under his skin.

He'd watched every video in the Keegans' library,
from *The Sound of Music* to *The Hunt for Red October,* right down to the last World War II training film,
read every book he was even faintly interested in, and
some he was not, and nothing helped. He was restless
as a ball of spit on a red-hot stove.

Dammit, even without trying, she was ruining everything!

* * *

After two days of clear, mild weather, the high-pressure area that had been holding a low one at bay shifted. The jet stream dipped, and the temperature dropped twenty-two degrees in six hours. Brace figured he'd better go check out the furnace at Blackbeard's Hole. While he was there, he might as well see if she needed any supplies. The last thing he needed was to have her take out one of the boats and run into trouble again. And knowing Frances, she'd starve before she'd ask for help.

Not that a woman who could turn a bunch of tasteless vegetables into a meal fit for a king was in any real danger of starvation. Matter of fact, while he was over on Hatteras, he might pick up some oysters and see what she could do with those.

Brace prided himself that he knew his way around a kitchen as well as most men. He'd been on his own for too long not to have mastered the can opener, both electric and manual. All the same, once a guy passed forty, it didn't hurt to start watching what he ate. Sodium—saturated fat...some of that stuff was supposed to be bad for you. A little professional help with his diet might not be a bad idea.

Yeah, and when a guy couldn't come up with a better excuse than that to see a woman, he was already in deep...gravy.

She met him halfway, her shimmery black hair blowing wild in the cold wind. "Hi! I made too much meatless lasagna last night, and I was wondering if you could help me finish it off. I spent a small fortune on all that mozzarella, too."

Damned if she didn't look shy! Who'd have thought a classy woman with a Katherine Hepburn style of beauty could look shy?

"Tell you what—if you'll let me provide the makings, I'll sign on as your guinea pig again. I'll even provide my own Maalox."

"It's a deal!" Frances told herself it was easier to cook for two than for one. And he still needed fattening up. And judging by what she'd seen of his culinary skills, sooner or later he would have poisoned himself. His idea of a meal was opening whatever can was handiest, lacing it with enough hot sauce to start a fire and enough salt to put one out, and then following it up with a king-size shot of antacid.

He didn't have to know that her manuscript was finished, and she had no more need for a guinea pig.

The first night of the new regime, they ate fat-free stir-fry and mounds of brown rice, and Brace looked hopefully for a salt shaker. Finding none, he shrugged and cleaned off his plate. Twice.

They played cards until midnight and warily traded a few secrets. Frances confessed to being a guilt junkie. "I'm not sure if it's a woman thing or a Catholic thing or if it comes from being the eldest of a large family, but I'm determined to break the habit."

Brace, who had confessed to a weakness for sucking oranges through a peppermint stick, asked, "What kind of guilt?" He was still smarting from losing three tricks in a row.

"Any kind. You name it. The car won't start? My fault. I should've taken it in for a checkup the minute it started to wheeze. Can't find the morning paper? My fault. I should've waited for the paper boy and taken it from his hand—that way I wouldn't have had to climb up on the roof and poke it out of the gutter with a broom handle."

"You didn't."

"Scout's honor."

He dealt two new hands and fanned out his cards, feigning a lack of interest in anything but the game. "No kidding. Anything else?"

"Guiltwise? How about infidelity?"

Brace's neat fan of cards exploded across the table. *"You?"*

"No, dammit, not me!" she growled. "Look, forget I said it, all right? Three cups of hot chocolate and I gabble like a turkey! Well? Are you going to pick up your cards and continue the game or not?"

They continued the game. Halfway through, Frances said, "And anyway, your confession was penny ante stuff. You owe me something a lot juicier than peppermint candy and oranges."

"You don't think that's juicy enough, huh? Okay—how about this. Once I stole four hubcaps, sold three, returned the fourth to the owner and collected a reward for my honesty."

"You didn't."

"Scout's honor." He mocked her earlier assurance.

"I doubt if you'd recognize a Boy Scout if you saw one," she scoffed.

"Wrong! I was a legitimate, card-carrying member of the Boy Scouts of America for nearly two weeks."

"That long, huh," she teased, her eyes sparkling in a way that made him wonder just when his sense of survival had ejected and left him three thousand feet up without a 'chute. "What happened? Did you steal the scoutmaster's merit badges?"

"I didn't see any badges I particularly wanted, so I made a pass at his wife."

She choked back a laugh. "You didn't!"

"Scout's—"

"Don't say it!"

Brace wondered idly how the sound of a woman's laughter could peg a man's temperature into the red and cause his head to spin like an altimeter in a power dive. It occurred to him that it had been a long time—like maybe never—since he'd felt this way with a woman.

Back off, man! This is one model you're not rated for.

On the other hand, maybe if he made a pass and she slapped him down, it would put things into perspective. At least he'd be back in familiar territory.

Only what if she didn't slap him down?

Yeah . . . what then?

When she took the last trick, he shoved his remaining pennies across the table and stood up. Tugging the collar of his black flannel shirt from his neck, he stretched and then sauntered over to check the thermostat. A bit too casually, he glanced at his watch. "Jeez, will you look at the time! I plan to run over to Hatteras first thing tomorrow, so if you think of anything you need, just make out a list."

"Sure. Thanks. I'll do that." He didn't offer to take her with him, Frances thought. She watched him grab his coat and stride out into the night, still struggling to ram his arms into the sleeves.

Before she could close the door, he was back. Her mouth was still hanging open when he caught her in his arms, which made it pathetically easy to plunder her sweetness. The kiss was hard and brief, but so thor-

ough they were both reeling from it a moment later
when he released her. His eyes burned into hers for a
small eternity, and then he wheeled away, back ram-
rod stiff, hands rammed in his pockets.

"Brace—wait!"

He didn't even slow down.

Unable to sleep, Frances was up and dressed when
she heard the sound of an outboard crank up early the
next morning. She grabbed her coat, her shopping list
and her purse and raced down the path toward the
harbor. "Hey! Wait up! I thought you were going to
wait for me!"

His greeting was marginally more cordial than a bear
coming out of hibernation. "I told you to make out a
list," he growled.

"I made one." She waved the lined page, ripped
from a spiral notebook, under his nose and jerked it
back when he reached for it.

Despite the cold, clear light of day, the memory of
that kiss hung between them, impossible to ignore.

Each was determined to ignore it. Brace reached for
her list again, but Frances shook her head. "I'm going
with you. I need to pick up a few things at the drug-
store."

"Add 'em to your list."

"Personal things," she snapped. He didn't want her.
She had fed him and laughed with him and spent hours
playing cards and trading silly secrets with him. He had
turned her entire world inside out with a kiss that had
blistered the soles of her feet—and now he'd reverted
to old Flint-Face. "What's wrong with you this morning? Indigestion?" she asked sweetly.

"Ah, hell— Just get in, dammit, I haven't got all day!"

Struggling against the desire to strangle him with his big sheepskin-lined collar, she marched down the pier and lowered herself into the runabout, taking a seat in the bow.

"Do you know what they say about people who use profanity all the time? They say your vocabulary is inadequate."

He wasted half a minute proving just how adequate his vocabulary was, and then he snarled at her. "Make yourself useful, will you? Let go the bowline."

She could have told him what to do with his bowline, but she didn't. Men! To think she'd almost started to like this one!

Almost? She'd been awake half the night, reliving that kiss—and worse—picturing that lean, powerful body in the altogether, wondering what it would feel like to explore it. Wondering how a man who looked as if he'd been put together from spare parts could turn her on with no more than a lopsided grin and a kiss that was over almost before it began.

Wondering why a man who was tough as old boot soles, a man who didn't like her any more than she liked him, a man who obviously didn't want her here, would bother to kiss her. How he could care for her so tenderly at a time when she was unable to care for herself. It was more than Kenneth had ever done for her, and once upon a time, Kenneth had claimed to love her.

But then, Kenneth had been a liar. Whatever else Brace Ridgeway was—and she suspected that there were things about him that would shock her to the very core of her small-town soul—he was basically an honest man. If he thought a woman was a fool, he said so. If he disliked her, he didn't bother to hide it.

If he wanted to kiss a woman, he did it. If he wanted to take her to bed, would he do that, too?

Oh, for pity's sake, at thirty-nine and a third, you'd have thought she was too old for fantasies. Or was this just one more lousy stage in a woman's emotional development? Post-post-adolescence!

Brace veered past the channel marker, cut the throttle as he neared the breakwater and idled up alongside the wharf. Even before they'd left Coronoke harbor, that damned conscience of his had kicked in. He'd managed to get through all these years without even knowing the thing existed, so why the devil did it have to rise up to haunt him now?

At least he was sleeping through the nights. No more nightmares. No more waking up screaming in the darkness, hearing that god-awful silence where there ought to be the roar of twin jets.

Lately he'd been waking up in a cold sweat from another kind of dream. The X-rated variety. Featuring a long-stemmed, black-haired woman with eyes like crushed violets, a tongue that could raise welts at fifty paces and a pair of small, pear-shaped breasts with delicate pale pink tips he would have sold his soul, if he even possessed such an organ, to taste just once.

Trouble was he was beginning to suspect that once wouldn't be enough. And that was scary as hell for a man who, except for one regrettable lapse, had never allowed any woman to come within striking distance since he was five years old and found out that kids could be returned like any other unwanted merchandise.

And then Sharon had had to call again. He'd just gone to bed after a shot of Keegan's bourbon, trying to put the woman and the kiss in perspective, when the phone had rung. It had been Sharon, wanting him to drive up and join a house party in Virginia.

He'd declined and hung up. She'd called back. He'd hung up again and then left the phone off the hook. That had taken care of Sharon.

This woman wasn't so easy to deal with. "Will an hour be enough time?" he growled, whipping a bowline around the nearest piling.

Frances, bristling at his tone of voice, scrambled up unassisted. It was an undignified exercise, at best, but not for all the gold at Fort Knox would she have asked for his help. "An hour's just fine." So she'd forego the pharmacy, which was several miles up the beach. If she couldn't find what she needed at the Red and White in Hatteras, she'd do without. She could always condition her hair with mayonnaise—although she wasn't sure the fat-free kind worked as well.

"Are you going to hang around all day staring at the water?"

"I'm waiting for you to get finished tying up the boat." And wishing she could jerk a knot in him! Would an ordinary good-morning smile kill him? Or even a polite "How are you?" Dammit, she'd thought they were getting along so well, and then he'd had to go and kiss her! She would almost rather do without the kiss than lose what little headway they'd managed to make toward friendship. Why did men have to be so blessed moody?

Kenneth had been moody, too. Maybe all men were. Not until two years after he'd died, when she'd learned about the double life he'd been leading, had she understood what was behind all his sudden, inexplicable mood shifts. It must've been rough, juggling a job, a mistress—and maybe even a son—with a wife. Even an incredibly gullible wife. All within a radius of thirty miles. And as if that hadn't been bad enough, half the town, including his parents, had been in on his dirty little secret!

Poor Kenny. The stress must've been horrendous, she thought now with a small, sad smile.

Brace saw the smile and quickly glanced away. Wordlessly they rounded the marina office. In the parking lot Frances unlocked her car; Brace unlocked his. She followed him to the Red and White and ignored him while she stocked up on groceries and the toiletries she needed.

There were few customers in the store—two clerks, a man in the meat department and a woman looking over the videos. Brace bought two bottles of catsup, two of tabasco sauce, half a dozen cans each of chili, pork and beans, macaroni and three of corned beef. Plus a giant bottle of antacid.

Next in line at the cashier, Frances eyed the antacid and snickered. If looks could have killed, she'd have dropped dead on the spot.

It was a seasonal town. Few businesses were open in early February. Frances loaded her own car while Brace loaded his. She followed him to the nearby post office, asked at the window for her mail—there wasn't any—and left before he could ask for his.

He came out empty-handed while she was backing out of the parking lot, and she waited. He led the procession—her old Chevvie and his sleek black whatsit—toward the marina.

They hadn't gone a thousand feet when a dog dashed out of the bushes on the side of the road. Frances hit the brakes, heart pounding, and the mongrel disappeared into a small wooded graveyard on the other side.

For some reason she was reminded of a wild puppy one of the kids had dragged home years ago. Every single one of the Smiths had been prone to rescue injured animals, usually leaving their care to Frances once the novelty wore off. She had nursed any number of unfledged birds, homeless kittens, starving dogs— and once two sickly goldfish that had been destined for flushing.

The wild pup had been found underneath a house that was about to be demolished. A workman had wrapped it securely in a scrap of blanket and given it to Reba, who had promptly handed it over to Frances. The flea-bitten wretch had snapped at everyone who'd attempted to feed him, much less pet him. After the first few days she'd been almost ready to call the animal control people; then the poor thing had escaped from the makeshift pen and had run out onto the street just as the garbage truck had rounded the corner.

The kids had cried. Even Frances had shed a tear or two. They had wrapped him in a faded crocheted rug and buried him out beside the birdbath. Debbie had reverently laid a dog biscuit on the small mound of earth, and Reba had transplanted a tulip bulb from the front yard. The dog biscuit had outlasted the tulip. Reba was not known for her green thumb.

Frances blinked. Oh, for heaven's sake, what on earth had gotten her to thinking about that poor wild puppy? She put him firmly from her mind, and a few minutes later she handed her sacks down to Brace and climbed unassisted into the runabout.

Wariness. It wasn't hard to recognize, not for a woman who had learned to be wary the hard way. The graveyard mongrel, the feral puppy and the man at the helm had a lot in common.

Seven

Finally! It was finished. Yet instead of a sense of accomplishment, Frances felt a distinct letdown. It was finished. So now what? Read the classifieds, look for a job, look for an apartment and start all over again. Somehow the brave new future that had looked so promising only a week or so ago was beginning to feel more and more like being out on a limb.

Methodically she put away the charts she had used to calculate the calorie content, the fat grams, both saturated and unsaturated, the fiber, vitamin and mineral content of each recipe included in *Fancy's Fat-Free Favorites*.

"Nice title...Fancy," Brace said. He'd been calling her that for several days now, ever since he'd seen the heading on the first few pages of her manuscript.

"My boss at the magazine thought Fancy had a ring to it, and Frances sounded fuddy-duddy." She was still a bit wary but determined to behave like an adult. If he could ignore that kiss, then so could she. "He said as long as we didn't run my picture with the column, nobody had to know how plain Fancy really was. So we used it and it sort of caught on."

Brace had come by to drop off a letter from her Uncle Seymore. He acted as if they were no more than casual acquaintances. Or maybe friendly enemies. Leaning against the paneled wall, he lifted his good eyebrow and studied her for a moment. "Oh, I don't know...maybe not fancy, but hardly plain."

It was a lukewarm compliment, even from him, but probably more than she deserved at the moment. She was wearing her oldest pair of slacks and a faded purple velour top Debbie had left behind when she'd moved to Texas. Her face was scrubbed clean, and her freshly shampooed and conditioned hair was still dripping down the back of her neck.

Deliberately she let her gaze linger on his windblown hair, the ancient sweatshirt and faded jeans he wore with his thick-soled boots. Why was it that when a man dressed casually, he looked masculine and downright sexy, yet when a woman dressed the same way, she was a slob?

Ken's favorite at-home costume had consisted of a pair of plaid Bermuda shorts worn with black ankle socks and bedroom slippers. About as sexy and masculine as a damp dish towel.

"Thanks for the newspapers," she said. She'd mentioned wanting to pick up as many as possible, and along with her mail he'd brought over copies of the *Raleigh News and Observer,* the *Norfolk Virginian Pilot and Ledger Dispatch* and a back issue of Keegan's *Hartford Courant.*

It was a start. She'd considered trying for something closer to Debbie or Reba, but neither of them was permanently settled, and she'd just as soon not find herself stranded a thousand miles from everything familiar.

Brace picked up a handful of index cards and leafed through them. "Olives? You mean my favorite green vegetable contains fat?"

"If that's your favorite green vegetable, it's a wonder you're so skinny."

"Look who's talking," he jeered, but it wasn't an unfriendly jeer.

Frances had been seated at the kitchen table when he'd let himself in, and now he leaned over her, bracing an arm on either side of her shoulders as he peered at a headline in the three-day-old *News and Observer*.

Nervously she shoved her hair back off her forehead, wishing he'd move away. She could actually feel the heat of his body. At a guess she'd say he burned roughly four thousand calories a day lying flat on his back. For all his seeming lack of energy, there was a coiled-spring tension about the man that was more than a little unnerving.

"Did you see this piece about the congressman and his little junket to the South of France? Claims the young lady was his cousin—he took her along only because she spoke French."

At the moment Frances wasn't certain she could manage plain English. His hand had accidentally brushed against her shoulder and lingered there. It didn't mean anything, but she wished he'd move away so she could resume breathing.

She leaned away, but his hand remained on her shoulder, his fingers warm and heavy as his thumb moved closer to the base of her throat. "Umm . . . I'd better go, uh—" she blurted.

Go where? Do what? She refused to fall apart again, just because a man was touching her!

"By the way, I had a card from Maudie," he said, his voice a soft rumble that raised gooseflesh down her arms.

"Maudie?" She edged away, and Brace stepped back. She told herself it wasn't disappointment she was feeling and knew it for a lie.

He was standing no more than three feet away, thumbs hooked under his belt, looking at her hungrily. As if he were starving and she was a crown roast complete with paper frills.

Which only showed how stress could affect a woman's judgement. "I was supposed to connect with a Maudie when I got here," she said with a brittle smile. "Uncle Seymore said someone called Maudie would show me the ropes."

Brace chuckled, and the sound played on her nerves like a chamber orchestra cellist. "And instead, you got me. I'm afraid I wasn't particularly nice to you that first day."

The brittleness faded and the smile became genuine. "Nor the second, nor the third—"

"Hey, give me credit for holding the bucket, at least. And don't forget those hunters."

He sounded amused. Frances almost wished he'd snarl at her again. She could deal with snarling a lot better than she could deal with these Jekyll and Hyde games he was playing. She'd never been any good at games. "Look, thanks for the mail and the papers, Brace," she said with determined cheerfulness. "But I'm sure you have better things to do than—than—"

"Fancy," he said softly. "Come here."

"The weather's really gone crazy, hasn't it? Hot one day, cold the next. Honestly, I've never seen such..."

She shoved back her chair, determined to get rid of him before she did something irreparably foolish.

She might as well have saved her energy. "Fancy, come here."

It was an order. If she obeyed, they both knew where it would lead. He'd kiss her again and she would kiss him back, and he'd know...

Brace didn't move. Frances couldn't. She drew in a ragged breath and tasted the tang of cold salt air and the subtle essence of warm masculinity. "Brace? What are you trying to do to me?"

"You have to ask?"

"I think one of us had better."

He stared at her for a long time, and then, with every evidence of reluctance, he stepped back, allowing her her freedom. "Yeah. Maybe you're right." His eyes were the eyes of a predator, his voice the purr of a mountain lion, but he didn't touch her. Instead he crossed his arms over his chest and stared moodily at the toe of his boot.

Trying hard to convince herself she was glad of the reprieve, she made a big production of restacking the index cards that held her recipe collection. Not even to herself would she admit how desperately she wanted to feel his arms again—to taste his lips.

Dammit, woman, Brace Ridgeway is only a fleeting moment in your miserable little existence—a tiny ripple on the sea of life!

A tiny ripple? Ha! The man was a blooming tidal wave! "Look, thanks again for the papers, Brace. I'll finish with them tonight and get them back to you tomorrow.''

He shook his head, and she didn't know whether it meant he didn't want them back or he was fed up with her again. And then he pulled that Jekyll and Hyde switch and smiled at her. Watching that tough, patchwork face—a face centered by an impossibly perfect nose—crinkle into a heart-breakingly beautiful smile, the last of her resistance melted and Frances knew she'd done it again. Heaven help her, when she set out to make a fool of herself, she did it in grand style!

''Am I forgiven?''

''Forgiven?'' she repeated weakly.

''For being a jerk.''

''Oh. Well . . . I don't suppose you can help it.''

''Ouch,'' he said softly, still grinning.

''Anyway, it's nothing to me, but I do wish you'd make up your mind whether I'm friend or foe, because it gets a little tiresome, trying to figure out whether to feed you or run for cover.''

''You're offering me a choice? Then I say we settle for friends. It's a beginning.''

A beginning? ''Well, I suppose if that's what you want. Anyway,'' she said, hedging a bet she didn't stand a snowball's chance of winning, ''I'll be leaving soon.'' She paused, and when he didn't fall on his knees and beg her to stay, she went on, her voice brittle with false cheerfulness. ''So maybe we can manage not to get on each other's nerves too much until then.''

Watching the color come and go in her translucent skin, Brace leaned his shoulders against the wall. Uncrossing his arms, he hooked his thumbs under his belt again. Don't count on it, lady, he thought. He'd never had a female friend—never wanted one. And whatever it was he wanted from Plain Fancy Smith Jones, he was pretty sure it wasn't friendship.

However, friendship would do for a start. It would do until he could figure out what there was about this one ordinary woman who had burrowed under his skin until he couldn't get her off his mind, asleep or awake.

That night he had another X-rated dream. He was reaching for the sun in an old World War II fighter. The P-39 was a single-seater with the engine behind the cockpit, yet somehow, she was behind him, nude except for a 'chute. With the illogical logic of dreams, he was able to see every delectable inch of her long, lean body as he pulled back the stick and took dead aim at the sun. Even over the roar of the Allison V-12, he could hear her laughter, and it was so warm, so real, so joyous, that he woke up with the sound ringing in his ears and a throbbing erection that took a hard set of calisthenics plus a long, cold shower to tame.

Now, jogging along the water's edge on the hard-packed sand, Brace completed the run around the perimeter of the island, veering inland only when he reached the marshy northeast end. He glanced at the time. Twelve minutes until the hourly newscast. Cutting through the woods, he maintained his pace until he neared the fifth cottage, the one on the end. The one with the green-and-white striped storm blinds.

Her place.

So much for clearing his head.

Determined not to get in any deeper than he already was, for the simple reason that he wanted to—wanted it so damned much he could taste it—he kept on going. Maybe a rundown on the current international brushfires, the beltway comedy and the stock market's latest paranoia would get her off his mind.

Yeah, and maybe pigs could waltz.

He poured himself a mug of coffee and sprawled in the big leather chair, sweaty but not even slightly winded. For a guy just out of the repair shop, he was in pretty good shape.

He switched on the radio and found a news station. Another fuse had been lit in the Middle East. Another congressman was trying to explain away his latest lapse of integrity. The market was down thirty-one points and falling, gold was up seven, and there was a line of thunderstorms moving east that had bombarded the western part of the state with baseball-size hail and flash floods.

Still restless, he switched off the radio and prowled the bookshelves. He flipped through a flying magazine, found it didn't hold his interest, cocked his head at the sound of a Cessna 172 flying low overhead and sighed. Maybe he should go warn her about the possibility of falling weather. She'd probably have her nose so deep in her recipes she wouldn't come up for air all day.

Fancy. With a reluctant grin, Brace shook his head, remembering her tone of voice when she'd said her boss had called her plain. She was about as plain as the high-performance engine he'd been testing when he'd lost it. Elegance personified. Sleek, clean, built for speed and endurance. That was Ms. F. Smith Jones.

Swearing softly, he rammed the old Mitchell B-25 video into the slot and settled down to refly the famous bombing mission with Doolittle's Raiders. Funny thing, coincidence. The B-25 had been named after General Billy Mitchell, who had proved his theory that planes could sink ships only a few miles offshore from this very island.

And now, some seventy-odd years later, not one, but two busted-up ex-fliers had ended up down here on a scrap of an island so small few people had ever heard of it.

Or maybe he'd been drawn here for another reason....

Frances had cooked enough spaghetti for two, considered taking a plate over to the Hunt and then reconsidered. Brace hadn't been by all day. She'd seen him only once since he'd brought the papers and the letter from Uncle Seymore. He'd jogged past that morning without even glancing her way.

So much for friendship. He obviously had even more of a problem with trusting than she did.

Thunder rumbled in the distance, and she wondered why she had included her tape player among the things she'd put in storage until she could find a place to resettle. A little Mozart would come in handy about now to cover the sound.

Or even a little Lawrence Welk. At this point she wasn't all that particular. Not that she was actually afraid of a little thunder. Snakes, yes. Snakes were sneaky, and they could bite. But noise couldn't really hurt you, and the chance of being struck by lightning was roughly a zillion and a half to one.

Nervously she switched on the television, tuned through a dozen or so empty channels and cut it off again. Cable didn't extend to Coronoke. The Keegans had had a satellite dish installed, but a high tide had done something or other to upset some gizmo, and according to Brace, they probably wouldn't be able to get it repaired until summer.

The days were getting noticeably longer, but because of the cloud cover, dark fell early. Frances switched on two lamps and the overhead fixture. Whistling tunelessly to keep up her spirits, she washed her few dishes and thought again about taking a plate of spaghetti and a salad to Brace, but at the sound of rain striking the side of the house, reconsidered.

Rain? It sounded more like hail!

The lights flickered once and she eased herself into the big chair, drew her feet up beside her and tried to remember everything she'd been told about the generator.

She'd been told she probably wouldn't need it. Period.

They flickered again, hung at half power for several seconds, then blazed up and went off.

For fully two minutes Frances sat without moving. Watching the almost continuous lightning through the windows, she tried to sort out light from sound and calculate the distance the storm was from Coronoke. Anything to occupy her mind.

"Thousand nine, thousand ten, thousand—"

A giant flashbulb went off in her face. At the same instant, a blast of sound made the hair on her arms prickle. Suddenly the air was filled with the smell of raw pine and ozone, and she covered her head with her arms and began to whimper.

"Oh, God, make it go away," she whispered. With no one to be brave for, she no longer had to pretend.

By the time Brace found her, she was cowering in the pantry. He came in the back door, having found the front blocked by the big pine that had been blasted by lightning. "Hey, are you all right?"

Frances stared at him mutely from her hiding place between the heat pump and the cleaning closet. He was drenched to the skin, wet clothes clinging to his lean frame, wet hair plastered over his brow. In the light of the hurricane candle lamp, the hard planes of his face looked even harder.

He was the most beautiful thing she had ever seen in her life, and without a second thought, she launched herself at him, too frightened to be embarrassed.

"Thank God you're here, Brace—I think it hit the house! Something exploded and then I smelled this rosiny smell and then— "

"Easy now, easy."

"Would you just listen to me? It hit the house! Brace, I heard it—I *felt* it!"

She was clutching his collar, half strangling him, and he forced her fingers free, covering them with his own. They were ice cold. "Shh, slow down now, it's all right, baby, everything's all right now."

"But I'm trying to tell you, there was this awful explosion and then—do you smell smoke? Oh, God, what if the roof's on fire?"

"Nothing's on fire, Fancy, but if it'll make you feel any better, I'll check it out." He turned away, but she caught his arm.

"Yes, please—only not now. Wait until it's over."

With a peculiar look born of amusement, frustration and an unexpected, raw-edged kind of hunger, Brace accepted the inevitable. Gathering her in his arms, he stroked her back and heroically resisted the temptation to spread his palms over her buttocks and press her against the throbbing ache in his groin.

"I'm getting you all wet," he rumbled against the top of her head. She was a tall woman, but he was taller. She fit him perfectly. *Too* perfectly!

When the power had gone off, Brace had switched on the generator at the Hunt. Evidently it hadn't occurred to her to do the same. At least she'd had the presence of mind to locate a candle. The dim, flickering light silvered the crooked tear tracks on her pale cheeks, and tenderly, he thumbed them away, acutely aware of the steamy heat being generated by two hot bodies and one set of wet clothes.

Even more aware of a need to comfort. "Come on now, honey, there's nothing to be afraid of. Storm's already miles away, probably out over the ocean by now." He inhaled deeply of her scent—that warm, grassy-spicy smell that was feminine without being the least bit cloying. His arms tightened. He buried his face in her hair and breathed in again, and suddenly he realized that her nipples were rock hard.

Judas priest, he didn't need this! Did she even know what was happening to them?

Hell, she had to know. She was no inexperienced kid—she'd been married. It was happening to her, too—unless those rigid nipples of hers had come from being plastered up against his wet shirt.

"Frances? Fancy," he murmured.

"This is crazy. Brace, I'm not usually so childish, honestly. It's just that—"

"That being alone in the dark in a strange house, on a strange island, knowing 911 can't help you if you need help. Yeah, I know, baby, I know. You don't have to explain anything."

Maybe not, but Frances desperately needed to explain it to herself. This simply wasn't like her. She was the one who'd always had to explain away all the things that went bump in the night. There wasn't an excuse in the world to hang onto a pair of wide, comforting shoulders now that the immediate danger had passed.

Except for the fact that she couldn't think of anywhere she'd rather be than here in his arms. Here in the strong, sheltering arms of a man who had done his best to drive her off, a man who refused to allow anyone to get close to him—a man who blew hot one moment, cold the next....

But who was definitely blowing hot right now.

She drew back and he allowed it, but he held on to her shoulders. "You're right," she said shakily. "There's nothing at all to be afraid of, except making a fool of myself." She managed an unconvincing laugh. "No novelty in that. It's one of my few real talents."

With the candlelight emphasising his beautiful nose and the oddly attractive patchwork of his other features, he smiled down at her, bringing her knotted fists up to his chest. "Why do I find that hard to believe? Aren't you the lady who pilots her own outboard, who writes books that are bound to wind up on the *New York Times Bestseller List?* Who—"

"My cookbook? Hardly!"

"Hey, don't stop me, I'm on a roll," he said, his voice caressing her nerves like a velvet mitt. "The lady who can make vegetables taste almost like real food?"

Food. Back to the real world, and just in time. Frances pulled her hands free and held them behind her back. "Yes, well…it's time for this multitalented lady to come out of hiding and start behaving like a grown-up again."

She almost made it, too. Would have, if it hadn't been for the storm's last kick. Lightning splatted so close the sound was instantaneous, and she hurled herself back into his arms. "Oh, God, I truly hate this," she cried, burying her face in his hard, wet chest. He laughed, and she lifted her head to glare at him. "It's not funny!"

"No. It's not funny," he said, sobering. "Not funny at all."

His face grew larger in the flickering light. Frances's eyelids grew heavy. The first kiss had been a fluke. Purely a matter of circumstances. The second was as inevitable as steel and magnets.

As for what followed, Frances blamed it on the storm—on all the electricity in the air. She blamed it on her battered self-esteem. She blamed it on anything and everything except the real reason, because she wasn't about to go proving, even to herself, that she'd done it again. Fallen in love with an impossible man.

His mouth was harder than it looked, yet incredibly gentle. The first kiss had ended almost before she'd had a chance to react. This time, he took it one slow, sweet step at a time, brushing her lips apart, nuzzling the corners of her mouth—giving her ample time to escape.

But escape was the last thing on her mind. When he came into her mouth, no longer trying to disguise the carnal nature of his intent, she opened eagerly, wanting all he could give her, needing to give that much and more.

Oh, she wanted him. Wanted him physically, wanted him emotionally—wanted desperately to reach out to the wounded creature she sensed behind that cool, baffling exterior. It was as if the hand on her breast that was setting off such an avalanche of sexual hunger had reached right inside her to touch her heart.

Brace dragged his mouth away and held her, breathing raggedly against her ear while he struggled to get his bearings again. Then, grabbing the candle in one hand and Frances with the other, he led her through the house to the bedroom.

Inside the room, he said with a look that was part wary, part amused, "I'm afraid I got you pretty damp." His own clothes were plastered to his body. Probably steaming by now.

"I'll dry," she whispered. If she didn't melt first.

All the air in the room must have suddenly been sucked out. She couldn't seem to catch her breath. She was shivering and burning up at the same time, and if he didn't hurry up and do something, she was going to come to her senses again, and heaven help her, that was the last thing she wanted to do.

Turning to the dresser, she ran trembling fingers through her hair. Brace moved behind her, wrapping his arms around her waist. When one hand moved up to close over her breast, she let her head fall back against his shoulder, moaning softly. The storm might have passed on, but she could have sworn lightning was still streaking through her body, from the nipple he was stroking with the pad of his thumb right down to her throbbing loins.

She could feel him thrusting against her bottom, hard and ready, and it inflamed her as nothing in her adult life ever had. How could she have lived this long without ever having experienced such intensity? Was it something to do with a woman's sexual maturity?

Or was it something to do with Brace?

He nuzzled her throat, causing her to gasp, and then he turned her slowly in his arms so that she was made achingly aware of how very much he wanted her. Hungrily, he kissed her again, and then somehow they found themselves more or less horizontal, a tangle of arms, legs and other more needy body parts.

Her lips parted eagerly under his fresh assault, and Brace took full advantage of her invitation. She tasted of cocoa and cinnamon and her own brand of sweetness. She tasted of aroused woman, and that was the greatest aphrodisiac of all.

She wanted him. Not the young stud he'd been twenty years ago, nor even the hotshot test pilot. She wanted him as he was now—a middle-aged reject with little to his credit but one perfect nose, a healthy bank balance and a slightly rusty degree in aeronautical engineering.

Memories faded in and out, like interference from a distant station. He shoved them aside. This was Frances, he reminded himself—not one of the eager beavers from his stunt-stud days. She was different.

Sure, but that didn't mean he was offering her anything more than he'd offered the others.

Or was he?

No, dammit, he wasn't! They were both consenting adults. She knew the score. Whatever personal baggage they were carrying, it had nothing to do with this. So they'd have tonight, and maybe a few more nights, and then she'd leave. And eventually he would, too. They could both look back on a few good memories, which was a hell of a lot more than most people ever had. So why not go for it?

His shirt was already unbuttoned. She helped slide it off his shoulders. He found the tail of the velvety top

she was wearing and worked it up over her breasts—
those beautiful breasts that he hadn't been able to forget. She'd been too miserable to know, and he'd been
too damned honorable to take advantage of the situation, but that didn't mean he'd forgotten.

On the dresser nearby, the candle lamp glowed
warmly. He'd brought it along for her sake. In case she
was afraid of the dark. As far as he was concerned,
he'd just as soon not shine any lights on his battered
carcass. Years of stunting and testing hadn't improved a body that had already borne the scars of
growing up on the streets.

He finished undressing, then eased her slacks down
over her hips. For all her leanness, she was remarkably well rounded where it counted. Somehow he was
certain that even if she'd been as scrawny as he'd first
suspected, he would have wanted her anyway. It was
the essential Frances who tempted him, rather than any
particular feature or attribute. And that alone, he told
himself, should've tripped his alarm system.

Knowing he wasn't about to back out now, Brace
forced himself to give her one last chance to do it for
him. "Fancy, listen—you understand, don't you, that
I'm not offering anything—"

"Did I ask you for anything?"

"No, but I thought maybe you—ah, hell, you know
what I'm trying to say."

Smooth, Ridgeway. Real smooth. Dammit, he didn't
want to turn her off, he just wanted to level with her.
He had a pretty good idea she was among the walking
wounded, and he'd have cut off his right arm right now
before he'd risk hurting her. There was always cold
showers. He could always stand out in a February

thunderstorm for a few hours. That ought to cure what ailed him.

Something told him he'd need more than a few hours, and that scared him a little, but not enough to bail out. "No, sweetheart, you didn't ask. I just don't want any misunderstandings between us. This is your first time since—well, since your husband died, isn't it?"

She was a widow, he reminded himself. A beautiful young widow who was even more on the defensive than he was. Odds were she'd been hurt pretty recently. She was still vulnerable, but she was as steamed up right now as he was.

So he'd take it slow and easy and make it good for her. She wouldn't regret it. That much he could offer her, at least.

Frances couldn't believe she was lying here in bed with a man she had never even known three weeks ago, calmly discussing her marital relations. "Look, Brace, if you've changed your mind and don't want to do it, just say so."

"Changed my mind? Honey, I want it so bad I'm only afraid I'll embarrass myself and disappoint you."

"Then why are we waiting?"

"To give you a chance to think, in case you want to bail out."

"I don't want to think," she said flatly.

"Yeah, me, neither," he said, trailing a forefinger over her chin, down her throat and between her breasts. "Right now I'm wondering why I don't shut up and get down to business."

Frances didn't know whether to weep or to hit him. "Brace, has anyone ever accused you of being a romantic?"

"Nope."

"Well, don't hold your breath."

And then she was holding hers. His roving forefinger was circling her navel now. He was lying on his side, propped up on one elbow with the dim light of the candle behind him. She was tempted to run her fingers through his thick hair, drying now in clumps, and pull. Hard!

Instead, she leaned over and bit him on the part closest to her mouth, which happened to be his chest. On a brown, hair-encircled male nipple, to be exact.

Brace yelped. With a soft oath, he lowered his face to her breast and returned the favor. Inhaling her warm fragrance, he warned himself again not to rush things. She was so damned fragile, and for some reason she affected him in a way no woman ever had.

She deserved to be pleasured. And dammit, if he never gave her anything else, he could give her that! He'd see to it that she had one hell of a fine memory to carry home with her when she left.

"I'm just trying not to rush things," he whispered in the curve of her throat, wanting desperately to rush things. He could feel her heart pounding, hear the little catch in her breathing, and it set him on fire, knowing that he was doing it to her. Suckling her breast, he used his tongue and his teeth, and she shut her eyes and gasped, her whole body stiffening out.

"Please," she whispered, shuddering as lightning streaked down from breast to loin. He was alarmingly aroused, yet she wasn't frightened. Never in her entire experience had she ever known any man so vitally, utterly...male!

She knew for certain that she had never felt so vitally, utterly—female!

With exquisite sensitivity, he explored her mouth, even as his hands explored her body. By the time his fingers parted her, she was wild with a heedless urgency that was tearing her apart. "Please, Brace—please..." she whimpered. She lifted her hips, practically begging him to end this exquisite agony, and still he hesitated.

"Sweetheart, you deserve a lot more than—"

"I don't *care* what I deserve, I only know what I want!"

This was plain, dull Frances Smith Jones? Yelling out demands in bed? She didn't even recognize herself! Tomorrow, or next year, when she was once more capable of coherent thought, she would probably tell herself that it was all Ken's fault, for years of unfaithfulness. She owed him this, even in retrospect.

But it wasn't Ken's fault. It wasn't even the fact that maybe once in her lifetime a woman simply needed to be irresponsible. It wasn't any of those things, it was the man himself. The man who was gazing down at her as if he could see clean through her soul. The man whose fingers were weaving their way through her pubic hair, who was even now kneeling over her, preparing to fill the emptiness inside her, to heal what ached and make her whole again.

Eight

If this is all I can have of him, Frances thought the instant before all rational thought fled, then let it go on forever—don't let it end too soon!

But there was no way to delay the inevitable. It had been too long for her—it had been too long for Brace. No sooner were they joined than the universe exploded. Brace uttered something that sounded suspiciously like a sob. He swore softly. And then he collapsed, his face buried in her shoulder.

For one moment Frances bore his full weight, her arms filled with his hard, sweaty body, her achingly aroused senses filled with the mingled aroma of sandalwood soap and healthy male flesh. And then he rolled away, and she was suddenly bereft. It was as if she'd been cast naked out into a cold rain.

She wanted to draw him back, to bury herself in his warm embrace, to be held at least until the aching emptiness went away, but she didn't. She refused to cling. Men hated women who clung. This man would hate it even more than most.

"I'm sorry. God, I'm sorry, Frances." There was a rawness to his voice that hadn't been there before.

Frances sighed. Not sweetheart. Not even Fancy. Just Frances. Plain Frances.

What did he have to apologize for? The fact that she'd been such a dismal failure that it had been over almost before it started? Or was he apologizing for taking her to bed at all?

Either way, she didn't want to hear it. With a sad little smile she reached down and dragged the covers up over her ears, feeling cold to the marrow of her bones. He slung one arm over her and pulled her to him, and she knew the exact instant he fell asleep. Long after his breathing grew deep and even, she lay awake, wondering what there was about her that made her so inadequate as a woman. Only one man had wanted her enough to take on her obligations—although by that time her obligations had been grown up and on their own, for the most part.

But even then she'd been so lacking in whatever it was a man wanted from a woman that his interest had quickly waned. According to his mother, Ken had been in love with that overdeveloped bimbo at the Hair Station before he and Frances had ever met, only Kiki had been married then. So Ken had married Frances, and then his little silicone goddess had been dumped by her husband and she'd started up with Ken again. The small detail of his marriage hadn't mattered at all. On Kiki's alimony, and with the help of Frances's salary, they'd had it all, Ken and his little Barbie doll. All the fun and none of the responsibility.

So much for learning from experience.

Carefully she rolled over to find Brace awake in the near darkness, his eyes reflecting the soft gleam of candlelight. Neither of them moved, neither of them spoke. The pale, flickering light was kind to his irregular features, yet nothing could disguise the fact that she'd gone to bed with a man she barely knew.

Frances Aldeana Smith Jones, a woman who had first preached abstinence and then caution to her younger sisters and then blithely disregarded the lessons of a lifetime for one brief moment of—

Of what? Love? It couldn't be love, because regardless of what her heart was screaming, her head told her that she didn't know this man well enough to love him. And if he had his way, she would never get close enough to know him any better.

"Second thoughts?" His gravelly whisper startled her into honesty.

"Lots of them." She could barely see his face, yet she could feel his eyes as they moved over every visible inch of her face. She was tempted to duck under the covers, but it was a little late for that.

"Not surprising. When a lady takes a lover for the first time—and it was the first time since your husband, wasn't it?" She nodded and caught the gleam of white teeth in his dark face. "She's entitled to something more than an aborted take-off."

"I wouldn't exactly call it taking a lover," she said dryly.

She didn't want to talk about it. People in the movies might talk about it afterward, but not the people in real life. With Ken it had been puff, pant, grunt, groan and snore. Friday nights and Wednesday nights, and then only Wednesday nights, and then not at all.

Job stress, he'd claimed. Meanwhile his little side dish had smirked every time Frances had walked into the shop. Kiki had consistently butchered her hair and then overcharged her for a style cut, and Frances, thanks to a combination of guilt because of her securely married status and pity for the struggling single parent, had stoically put up with it and come back for more.

And then consistently overtipped!

Well, so much for guilt, she thought now as she tried to ignore the hand that was straying back and forth over her hip. She was done with assuming personal guilt for everything from acid rain to the national debt.

"Fancy? You awake? I said I'm—"

"Look, you don't have to apologize. We're both old enough to know what we're doing. Surely we can—" She broke off with a gasp. "Brace, would you stop doing that? It tickles!"

"What tickles...this?" His fingers trailed down over the outside of her thigh, circled her knee and then moved back up the inside. "Or this?"

"Everything!"

"Why wouldn't you call us lovers?" He sounded lazily amused, which was the last thing in the world she felt. She felt...agitated. And mad as hell. She felt as if she'd been offered a four-course, five-star dinner, only to have it snatched away before she could even pick up her cocktail fork. She caught his hand and moved it away, and he leaned closer and blew softly against her throat.

"Because we're not," she snapped. "Just because we— Brace, don't do that!"

"Just because we what, Fancy?" He continued to explore with his hands and his lips while she struggled to maintain her composure. "We made love. That makes us lovers, doesn't it?"

"We had sex! That makes us nothing we weren't before we—"

"Made love?"

"Had sex!"

His head came up just as the candle guttered and flickered out. "Quit trying to sound so tough, will you? It's out of character."

"You don't know the first thing about me and my character, so stop trying to pretend you do. And you needn't bother to offer me any false promises, either, because I'm not exactly stupid!"

The hand on her breast grew still, and she brushed it away. Deliberately, he put it back, taunting her nipple as if to prove his power over her.

And he had that, all right. Power. While she was still desperately trying to reassert her common sense, he said, "Have I ever offered you anything?"

"No, but—"

"Right. And don't tell me I don't know you, lady, because I know a lot more about you than you think I do. For one thing, I know that what just happened was no good for you, and that's my fault. I'm sorry. I told you it'd been a long, dry spell for me."

"Yes, well..." Never in her life had Frances thought she'd ever be discussing something so intimate with a stranger. Before she could think of a rational comment, he went on.

"I also happen to know that underneath all that phony independence you strap on like an iron corset every morning, you're—"

"I don't—"

"You're hurting and you're scared, and you'd rather die than ask for help. I'm not sure who or what sent you into exile, but I'm damned well certain you're not cut out to fly solo."

"You don't know the first thing about—"

"You're used to being around people, right? At a guess, I'd say you're used to having people depend on you. You're the type who can be strong as long as her strength is needed, but the minute that need passes, you go somewhere private and quietly fall apart. Am I ringing any bells?"

Frances couldn't believe she was lying here in bed with a perfect stranger, both naked as the day they'd been born, discussing her character, her personality and her particular strengths and weaknesses. No one had ever dissected her quite so thoroughly, not even herself. It was a little scary. "Too many for comfort," she admitted with a small sob of laughter.

Brace's arm slipped over her shoulders and he tugged her closer, and because there was nowhere else in the world she would rather be, she allowed him to hold her. Just for a little while, she promised herself.

But then holding was no longer enough. With the storm long gone, the stars were beginning to come out. The warm, paneled bedroom smelled of cypress, soap, sex and candlewax, and her last rational thought was that no perfume in the world could be so provocative.

"This time's for you," Brace whispered.

This time was for both of them. He made love to her with a slow, soul-shattering thoroughness that left them both limp and dazed. By the time she dissolved in his arms, his taste was on her tongue, his scent in her nostrils, and her hands knew every rugged, battered inch of his lean, hard body.

And heaven help her, she was miles deep in love! Against all reason—against every lesson she had learned since Paul Capro had broken her heart by giving her a box of candy for her birthday instead of the engagement ring she'd expected, she was in love with a man she barely knew, a man who freely admitted that he wasn't offering her anything more than a brief sojourn in heaven.

Brace was in the shower, Frances in the kitchen, adding all sorts of sinful additions to her own virtuous granola mixture, when she heard the sound of an outboard.

"Brace? I think we might have company," she called through the open door. "Were you expecting anyone today?"

"Nope. Must be for you," he called back. Even the timbre of his voice had the power to turn her bones to jelly. She'd better pull herself together. Fast!

She measured decaf into the filter, the sound of the outboard forgotten. It was probably just a sightseer, anyway. Or maybe a fisherman. Sound traveled long distances on water when conditions were right, and conditions were perfect. *Everything* was perfect, she thought as she did a quick little shimmy-shake for sheer joy.

She was topping off two glasses with vegetable juice when Brace came up behind her and slipped his arms around her waist, nuzzling her throat. "Since you asked, I'll take mine with a shot of Tabasco, thanks."

"For breakfast?"

"I like my juice the same way I like my women," he murmured with a comically overdone leer. "Hot 'n' spicy."

"Oh, for pity's sake, I haven't heard that line since I was in junior high!"

"Yeah, but those guys were just showing off. I really mean it." He reached around her for her condiment tray, to which he had recently made a few additions, just as she turned in his arms and reached past him to open the refrigerator.

And then they both forgot what they were about to do and did something else altogether.

And would have done far more if it hadn't been for the sound of a rat-a-tat-tat on her front door. "I'd better get it," she whispered, reluctantly leaning back in his arms. Her face was flushed, her lips were swollen and her eyes glowed like wet amethysts. She couldn't resist one small kiss on his crooked eyebrow.

"Hurry back, will you? We've got some unfinished business to take care of." He let her go, his grin blatantly salacious. Leaning against the countertop, legs crossed at the ankle, arms crossed over his chest, he looked tough and sexy and altogether irresistible, scars, crooked cheekbones and all.

Her wobbly legs managed to carry her to the front door—just barely. She swung it open to find Jerry, the boy from the marina.

"Mornin', Miz Smith. Hey, you wouldn't know where Mr. Ridgeway is, would you? He's got a visitor, only he's not at the Hunt. Boat's still tied up, though, so I figger he's still around here some'res."

Brace appeared behind her. "Got a message for me, son?"

"Hi, Mr. Ridgeway. Sure do! Brought you a visitor." Jerry looked curiously from Brace to Frances and back again. "She said did I know where you were at, and I said sure, and she said to take her, so I did, only you weren't there, so I said lemme ask around."

From the garbled account, one word stood out clearly in Frances's mind, even as Brace, swearing softly, grabbed his shirt and shoved past her without a word.

She.

Sharon was at the Hunt. By the time Brace got there, he was coldly furious, but no longer surprised. Pete would have allowed him the time agreed upon, but Sharon was another matter. Two years older than her brother, she looked about twenty-two and harmless as a butterfly.

Looks were deceptive. Pete Bing's bald, bland facade hid a razor-sharp mind and a dogged determination. Sharon's beauty covered hard self-interest and very little more. She might not want him for herself any longer, but she damned well wanted him for Bing Aero—wanted what he knew about a certain top-priority project he'd been working on for a certain government contractor when he'd hung it up.

And he'd be parboiled in hell before she'd get it!

"Surprise," she said grimly, rising to meet him on the broad front deck of the sprawling restored hunting lodge.

He was surprised, all right. For once in her expensively catered life, his ex-fiancée looked lousy. "Sharon." He nodded warily. "You're pretty far off the beaten track, aren't you?"

She shrugged and indicated her luggage. It, like everything else about her, from the toes of her Italian lizard skin shoes to the top of her flawlessly groomed platinum hair, was top of the line. His mind darted back to a woman who wore baggy flannels and chain-store tops, and as often as not, no shoes at all, even in the dead of winter.

"My flight was canceled and while I was waiting to see if they could book me on another line, I saw an ad offering charters to the Outer Banks and acted on impulse."

"Yeah, sure you did." Sharon Bing had never made an impulsive move in her life, and they both knew it. Even her engagement to him had been calculated, he suspected. It sure as hell hadn't been a love match. That teary little episode outside his hospital room had probably been staged deliberately so that he'd break it off and save her the bother. She must've figured he was too bashed up to be of any value to the firm—much less to her.

Brace put her bags in his own room for now, vowing that before the day was over, she'd be off the island. He would send her packing right away, except for two things. He was curious to know what her pitch would be this time. And maybe he wanted to prove to himself that there was nothing left.

It didn't help that she looked like the devil. Even with those gray hollows around her eyes and the red flush on her cheeks, she looked better than most women could ever hope to look. Sharon had been born beautiful and learned quickly how to improve on nature.

Learned how to use it to her advantage, too.

"I need a drink," she drawled, collapsing in the best chair in the room.

"It's barely ten o'clock in the morning."

"Oh, for heaven's sake, when did you turn into such a sanctimonious bore? Don't forget, sweety, this is Sharon. I knew you back when, remember?"

"Yeah, I remember. Bourbon or brandy?"

She shuddered and unbuttoned the top button of her white silk blouse while he opened the liquor cabinet. "You know what I like."

"It's bourbon or brandy, or...uh...scuppernong wine. The Keegans aren't much for drinking. Maudie uses the wine for cooking and keeps the other stuff on hand for emergencies."

"Oh—the bourbon, I guess. Believe me, this is an emergency. That ham-fisted pilot nearly collapsed the nose gear setting us down on that miserable little landing strip! I'm going to get his license pulled—if he even has one," she added, viciously yanking a cushion from behind her and hurling it onto the floor.

"The charter line belongs to a friend of mine. He doesn't hire amateurs."

"Yes, well you can tell your *friend* for me that the FAA might be interested in—"

"Cut the crap, Sharon. It won't wash with me anymore. Now why don't you just tell me why you're really here before I ferry you back to Hatteras. I hope you made arrangements to get off the island before dark. The strip's not lighted." He poured her two fingers of Keegan's bourbon, making a mental note to replenish the stock before he left. Handing it over, he wondered what she'd done with the carat and a half blue-white he'd given her. Traded it in for something else, probably.

"Never mind what arrangements I've made. I'm here because you're here." She tried one of her high-power smiles on him, but the voltage was so low it flickered and died before it could take effect. As he continued to regard her with cool skepticism, the corners of her mouth drooped again. "All right, so I made a mistake when I broke off with you. If it will make you feel any better, I'll admit it. But dammit, Brace, you have to remember, I was in shock! I'd just seen you after your first operation, remember? Surely you're not still holding that against me? What I said when you were—I mean, after your—"

"When I was flat on my back in the surgical ward with my face held together with staples? Oh, hell, no, sugar, why would I hold that against you? After all, you did send flowers, didn't you?"

She'd sent three dozen roses with a note telling him she had to fly to the West Coast on business and wasn't sure when she'd be able to get back.

Having already overheard her conversation in the hallway outside his door, whatever illusions he'd still managed to hang on to had gone down in flames when he'd read that brief note—not even in her own handwriting. She'd dictated it over the phone to someone in the florist's shop.

And anyway, he was allergic to roses. She hadn't even remembered that much about him.

Now, studying the woman who had twisted him around her little finger and then hung him out to dry, Brace waited with an objective sort of curiosity for the pain to start.

Nothing. Not a twinge. But then, he'd already begun to suspect that he'd had little more invested in the relationship than she had.

Which wasn't to say her timing hadn't been lousy, because it damn well had.

By noon it was obvious that Sharon wasn't going anywhere. Brace had a pretty good idea what was wrong with her. The same thing that was wrong with half the population of the southeastern United States, according to the latest news report. The same bug that had bitten Fancy.

He wasn't about to move Sharon and her germs into Rich and Maudie's room, with Maudie's gear scattered around like leaves after a hard wind. Keegan had spent half his life in the service. Neatness was second nature to him. Evidently Maudie had never acquired the habit.

The guest wing was closed off for the season. Heat pump shut down, lines drained. There were four empty cottages standing idle, but Brace lacked the authority to put one in to service.

Besides, if he was any judge, his uninvited guest was going to be needing a lot more than a bed any minute now. After nursing Fancy through the same short-lived but hard-hitting virus, he figured he was a pretty good judge.

Of course, there was one other option....

Nah. He couldn't ask that of her. Sharon was his responsibility, not Fancy's. Not even in his wildest days had he ever shirked a responsibility.

But dammit, the minute she was on her feet again, she was out of here!

As a nurse Brace considered himself about a degree and a half off the bottom of the scale. As a patient Sharon didn't even rate that high. At least Fancy had managed to thank him for holding the bucket, mopping her off and dosing her with cola, crackers and headache pills, even while she was sick as a dog.

Sharon was a constant pain in the neck. She blamed him for everything. Between demands and complaints, she whined about having had to make a special trip just to track him down.

"Who asked you to? I thought you were enjoying a vacation. Didn't you say you were part of a house party?"

"Oh, for God's sake, since when do I have time for a vacation," she grumbled. She blamed him for her flu, because according to Sharon, there was no flu west of the Mississippi.

Brace bore it all with grim good cheer, knowing it wouldn't last much longer. It could've been worse. He could've been married to her.

The cold cloths were too cold and dripped on her pillow. Her tea was too hot and too strong, the toast was burned and the crackers were stale.

"It's hard to keep crackers crisp in this salt atmosphere," he snapped.

"For God's sake, stop yelling at me! Can't you see my head's splitting? I have to use the bathroom."

Resigned, he helped her to her feet. "Lean on me."

"Don't rush me, dammit! All the sensitivity of a rhinoceros! It's no wonder you can't fly! Where did you put my slippers?"

"I couldn't find any slippers."

"That stupid maid probably kept them for herself! Then buy me some, you have a telephone! Call Neiman Marcus and have them overnight several pairs in my size!"

"You'll be gone by the time they get here." Brace held her as if she were made of porcelain. She looked as fragile as bone china, but he happened to know she was about as fragile as an old combat boot.

"Dammit, Brace, quit trying to trip me up!"

"I'm not trying to trip you up," he said with barely concealed impatience. "If you'd quit trying to see yourself in the mirror—"

"My hair—"

"Your hair looks okay!"

"How would you know? The only time in your miserable life you ever displayed the least bit of sensitivity or good taste was when you asked me to marry you!" She slammed herself into the bathroom, and Brace stood outside the door, glowering at the innocent, polished-walnut panels.

She was in there studying herself in the mirror. He knew for a fact that she was congenitally incapable of passing one without admiring her reflection.

Unexpectedly his battered sense of humor began to emerge. He called through the door, "About your hair, honey—I didn't want to be the one to tell you that the varnish is cracked and the back's flat, and the rest is so tangled it's going to take a hay rake to sort it out. And about that zit on the back of your neck—"

Something crashed against the door, and he chuckled. A guy had to have some means of holding his own against the weaker sex.

Late the next evening Brace knocked on Frances's door. He hadn't seen her since the previous morning when Sharon had arrived. It occurred to him that there was nothing in the world he'd rather be doing at the moment—including flying—than sprawling in that big leather chair while she worked at the kitchen table on her manuscript. He could see her fingers flying over the keyboard, hear her muttering under her breath. She talked to herself while she worked, and he found the trait endearing. It occurred to him that he was beginning to find everything about the woman endearing, even her phony independence.

Especially her phony independence.

She opened the door and stood there, not exactly inviting him inside, but not slamming it in his face, either.

"Hi. Are you tied up?" Increasingly uncomfortable under her level regard, he found his smile hard to maintain.

"Why, did you need something?"

"No. Well, yeah—actually, I guess I do. Mind if I come inside for a few minutes?"

Frances had been getting dressed to run over to Hatteras, to see if her manuscript was ready to be mailed yet. She'd had two copies printed up, one for her, one for the editor. She'd planned to do some shopping while she was over there, maybe get her hair trimmed and then buy a few more newspapers to check out the classified sections. With the book finished, it was time she got on with making up her mind where to go from here, and that depended on where she could find the best job.

"If you're busy, I can come back later."

She stepped back, steeling herself against the rush of feelings just seeing him again had brought on. She'd had a day and a night to put things in perspective. One look at his beautiful nose, his crooked eyebrow and those fathomless gray eyes, and she had it all to do over again.

"Has your visitor left? She didn't stay long." Her smile was as phony as a four-dollar bill.

"Still here. Leaving tomorrow, though. The thing is, something's come up and I need to ask a favor."

She saw him hesitate and wondered if he felt as awkward as she did. What had happened between them had changed everything. Now they were neither friends nor enemies—certainly not the lovers he had claimed. In an unguarded moment, Frances found herself gazing into those wary gray eyes, and it hurt so much she wanted to strike out and hurt him as much as he was hurting her.

But she didn't. It wasn't in her nature. Once a doormat, always a doormat. "I'll be glad to help if I can, but I'm on my way to the marina at the moment. Could I do some shopping for you while I'm there?"

During a long, sleepless night, Frances had concluded that if the relationship between Brace and his anonymous "she" were completely innocent, he would have brought her over and introduced her before now.

He hadn't. "What happened, did you run out of food? If you need to borrow something, you're more than welcome to anything in my kitchen, but I'm afraid the cupboard's a little bare at the moment."

He wiped a film of sweat off his forehead. The temperature in the shade barely reached into the forties. "Look, I hate like the devil to ask you this, Fancy, but could Sharon borrow your spare room? It'll just be for one night." He looked about as uncomfortable as it was possible for a tough, enigmatic man to look when he habitually wore a suit of armor. "Rich and Maudie and the baby are on their way home right now. I'm scheduled to collect them in about forty-five minutes, and Sharon says she's not up to traveling yet. She's just getting over that flu thing you had."

The flu. Frances almost smiled. That explained a lot, but not everything. "You mean you had to play Florence Nightingale again? Poor Brace, that's rotten luck.''

"Dammit, Fancy, I need help!'' He raked his fingers through his hair, leaving it fork-lifted into untidy clumps.

Like butter and honey on hot waffles, something warm and sweet began to melt and flow through her veins. He needed her. Without knowing how she knew, Frances was certain that very few women, if any, had ever heard those words from Brace Ridgeway. Hardbitten, battle-scarred warriors weren't into admitting weaknesses, much less begging favors.

A slow smile set her dark violet eyes to dancing as she held the door wide. "You'd better come inside where it's warm and tell me about it.''

Nine

With the temperature hovering in the low forties, Brace felt the sweat begin to form on his face. Sharon had started in on him the minute he told her she'd either have to leave Coronoke or bunk in with a neighbor. He'd had to overcome his own strong sense of privacy when he'd moved into the Keegans' home in their absence. Inviting someone else to share it with him was out of the question. When the situation had suddenly gone south, he'd had little choice, but things were different now.

"It's not like there wasn't room," she carped. "How many rooms has this dump got, anyway? Two dozen? Three dozen?"

"Both wings are closed off for the winter. The whole island shuts down for the winter."

"Well, you're here, and evidently this other person is, so I don't see what difference it makes—"

"Come on, come on— Get a move on, will you?"

"Damn you, Ridgeway, I don't *want* to move in with some strange woman!"

"Call it a bed and breakfast and count your blessings. It's either that or a motel over on Hatteras—if you can find one still open."

"God, you're callous. How I could ever have even considered marrying you is a mystery to me. I must've been out of my mind!"

Brace didn't bother to reply. Barely masking his impatience, he hurried her along the sandy path, wondering sourly why any woman with enough brains to be CEO of a small but successful aircraft manufacturing outfit would be stupid enough to wear open-toed, slingbacked, three-inch heels to a place like Coronoke Island. If he had to put up with much more of her perpetual whining, he was going to crate her up and ship her back to Bing Aero via air freight!

"Why can't you go home with me? You've had plenty of time to think it over. We could charter to Norfolk and catch a flight out this afternoon and—"

"Forget it."

"But why do you have to stand guard on this dump? It's not as if there was anything here to steal."

"Watch out for that vine."

She kicked aside the briar vine that lay half-buried in the sand, and it snagged her nylon. Grimacing, she plucked it away. "Oh, yuk! Who is this person you're pushing me off on, anyway—Sheena, queen of the jungle?"

"Her name is Jones and she's down here finishing up a book."

"She's a writer? Is she a friend of the Keegans?"

"She's got a spare bed she's willing to lend you, okay? That's all you need to know. Now, will you get a move on? It's going to take me an hour to get up the beach to the airstrip," he snapped, and she cut him a speculative look as she plowed through the sand at his side.

As the muscles at the back of his neck solidified into case-hardened steel, Brace reminded himself that he'd once thought enough of this woman to ask her to marry him. She was the sister of a friend and business acquaintance. She'd been sick, and she still wasn't back up to par, and while wringing her neck might relieve his feelings, it wouldn't do much to improve the overall situation.

Frances opened the door. She'd changed out of her slacks and was wearing a dress in some peachy-pink color that reflected on her face, making her look flushed and so damn beautiful it hurt just to look at her. With a sinking feeling that he'd have done better to have made other arrangements—not that he'd had much choice—Brace made the introductions.

"Ms. Bing, Ms. Smith Jones. Uh—that is, Smith. Oh, hell— Fancy, this is Sharon." He tugged at his collar. If his back had been against a wall in front of a firing squad, he couldn't have felt any more desperate. "If you two will excuse me, I'd better head on up the beach."

"I haven't heard a plane fly over," Frances said.

"Yeah, well..." He shrugged and edged toward the door. "Don't want to keep 'em waiting. Baby might take cold."

"You're worried about a baby?" Sharon taunted. "That's a switch. I didn't know our famous stunt-stud ever worried about anyone but himself. Has he told

you his life story yet, Ms. Johnson? It's amazing what
you can find in department stores, isn't it?''

"Smith," Frances corrected absently. She looked
bewildered. Sharon looked smug. As for Brace, he
looked as if he might be toying with the idea of a little
genteel mayhem. When it came to mistakes, he'd made
just about every one in the books, but the worst mistake of his life had been getting involved with Sharon
Bing. The night they'd decided to get married—and to
this day, he wasn't quite sure who'd mentioned it
first—they'd celebrated by drinking each other under
the table. Brace had all but given up alcohol after
watching a fellow stunt pilot belt down a few and then
fly his chopper into the side of a grain silo.

But that night he'd celebrated big, and in a rare
mellow mood he'd let slip a few things about his past
that he'd never told another living soul.

Frances, conscious of the undercurrents, if not un-
derstanding them, stepped between her two guests and
urged Brace out the door. "Run along then, we'll be
just fine. I'm looking forward to finally meeting the
famous Maudie."

He wanted to wrap her up and tuck her away somewhere deep inside him, where nothing could ever hurt
her again. "I owe you," he said just low enough for her
ears, and she shook her head, smiling.

"You don't owe me anything." Nor did she owe him.
The score was even between them, and she intended to
see that it remained that way. No more dreaming foolish, dangerous dreams.

Both women watched him leave, then Frances said,
"I have some fat-free apple-yogurt coffee cake fresh
out of the oven, Miss Bing. Would you rather have tea
or coffee?''

* * *

Brace jogged down to the plank pier, feeling as if he'd just ejected with an untested 'chute and landed in the top of a tall, tall tree. So far, so good, but he still wasn't on the ground yet. The Keegans were back three weeks early. He was just now beginning to realize that in a couple of hours, he'd be excess baggage on Coronoke. He still hadn't figured out his next move. For the first week or so he'd just soaked up sleep and solitude, and then Fancy had shown up, and he'd had to deal with that. And then, just when he was beginning to get a handle on things, Sharon had dropped in out of the blue.

Since then he'd been so busy thinking of ways to get Sharon off his hands so that he could spend some serious time exploring this thing with Fancy, he hadn't had time to think of anything else.

Frances had never been good at people games. She wasn't even sure what game Sharon Bing was playing, but she had a pretty good idea which one of them was winning and which one was losing her shirt.

"It's really rather amusing, isn't it, the way poor Brace hustled me out of the house for the sake of appearances?"

"I thought it was so the baby wouldn't be exposed to the flu."

"Is that what he told you?" The blonde toyed with the loose band of her diamond-encrusted wrist watch. "I think the truth is, he's embarrassed to be caught playing house. Poor baby. It's really amusing when you think about it, because if there's one thing Bracewell is not, it's a prude. Believe me, I should know. Did he happen to tell you about that weekend we flew up to Dayton to this air show and got locked inside an am-

bulance for seven hours? That was the first time—
Well, I needn't go into that."

Amusing? That was the last word Frances would've
used to describe it. She said something polite and
clenched her fists until her nails dug into the palms of
her hands.

"Which is why it would never have occurred to me
he'd be embarrassed to have these friends of his know
I was sharing his bed, but then, who knows how the
masculine mind works? And Brace's mind, I do assure
you, is one hundred and fifty percent male. Just like
everything else about him." She leaned back and extended one leg, flexing her ankle to sift the loose sand
from her shoes onto the floor Frances had swept just
that morning. "I gather these Keegan people are
friends of yours?"

"I've never even met them."

"No? Then you're down here at Brace's invitation?"

"Not really. This cottage belongs to my uncle. I'm
only borrowing it for a while."

Sharon sipped her tea, wrinkled her nose and declined the coffee cake. "Brace says you're a writer."

"Not really. Well, I suppose so, but primarily, I'm a
nutritionist. I worked as a dietician at a hospital for
several years before I started editing a monthly column on food, and now I—"

"How fascinating."

Frances nibbled the large chunk of coffee cake she'd
cut for herself. It tasted like papier mâché with apples,
and she laid it on her napkin.

"What are your immediate plans?" Sharon asked.

"Plans? Well . . . now that my cookbook is finished,
I'm looking for another job as a dietician. I saw an ar-

ticle in a Virginia paper about vocational training—the old Home Ec. classes have changed beyond all recognition since I was in school—they include the commercial end as well as—"

Sharon yawned and clattered her cup in her saucer, and Frances could have bitten her tongue. Was there something lacking in her brain? Some vital nutrient missing from her diet that prevented her from learning a lesson no matter how many times she repeated it?

Shades of Kiki Bonhurst! "But you can't be interested in all that. Why don't I show you where everything is, and if there's anything else you need, you've only to ask. Meanwhile, I have things to do, so I'm sure you'll excuse me."

"You're too generous," the petite blonde purred, and Frances silently agreed. What she'd really like to do was pour the rest of the tea over that perfect platinum pageboy and then shut herself up in her bedroom and cry for a solid week!

Maudie Keegan was the kind of woman who instantly put everyone at ease. She stopped by the Seymore cottage late that afternoon and invited Frances and Sharon for a potluck supper, as it was Sharon's last night on Coronoke.

Which was the first Frances had heard of her leaving. She had a feeling it was the first Sharon had heard of it, too, although she had to give her credit. If Brace's blond friend was surprised, she covered it beautifully.

"Brace said you're a fantastic cook, Mrs. Jones."

"Frances, please. I'm in the process of going back to my maiden name, and it gets so confusing." She didn't know why she'd said that, other than that

Maudie was the kind of woman who invited confidences.

"And you may call me Sharon, Mrs. Keegan." Sharon Bing extended a small, square hand as if conferring a great favor.

Maudie perched on the arm of the lounge chair. She sniffed appreciatively. "Do I smell cinnamon buns? I haven't had one of those in years!"

"Coffee cake, made with fat-free yogurt and apples instead of shortening. Why not take it home with you? I've had all I want, and it'll just get stale."

"Oh, wonderful! There's nothing sweet in the house, and I know I won't have time to bake until I get unpacked."

"Are you sure you want us tonight?"

Maudie assured them she did. "I'm too tired to do anything tonight except relax and enjoy being home, and if you leave me to my own devices, I'll be unpacking and washing clothes all night."

A time was agreed on, and Frances promised to bring whatever she had on hand. "Brace said you probably would," Maudie admitted, and the two women laughed together.

Sharon said, "I'm afraid my talents lie in another direction. If you've a business that needs streamlining, I'm your woman. My specialty is efficiency— making every square inch profitable and every man on the payroll pull his weight." She turned her attention back to the nail she'd been filing. Maudie looked at Frances, shrugged and winked, and Frances grinned and walked her to the door with promises to see her later.

* * *

The table groaned under a miscellaneous feast, consisting of Frances's health food, Maudie's home-canned vegetables, Rich Keegan's smoked fish and Ann Mary's squashed chocolate fudge, brought all the way from Utah.

Brace was telling Rich Keegan about flying a biplane over a burning building while another stuntman hung from the struts. Maudie was fingering up chocolate crumbs and Frances was stacking dishes in the dishwasher when a sleepy wail sounded above the conversation.

Rich rose with an apologetic grin. "Call of the wild," he said laconically. "My turn, honey."

Sharon's expression said she was less than fascinated by all the evidence of domestic bliss. "God, I'd kill for a vodka martini right now," she muttered. "Brace, do you remember that— Bracewell? Wake up!"

But Brace wasn't asleep. Eyes slitted half shut, he was exploring the sense of deep contentment that had settled over the room in the past few hours. A lot of it had to do with Rich and Maudie Keegan, but not all. When Frances had walked through the door with a casserole in one arm and a basket over the other, something inside him had begun to thaw and break up, like an ice jam in the first warm days of spring.

He'd watched her all evening, but he hadn't found an opportunity to speak more than a few words. Not that it really mattered. Just being around her was enough for now. Watching the easy way she got along with Maudie and Rich—the way she was with the Chief, which was what the Keegans called their eleven-month-old son.

That really got to him. Remembering what she'd said about wanting children, knowing the clock was running out on her, he thought it was a damned shame. He thought a lot of things, not all of them particularly rational, but all of them exceedingly sweet to contemplate.

Gradually, though, watching her with Sharon, he gained a feeling that something was wrong. Dammit, if only Sharon hadn't showed up—if only the Keegans had held off a few days, he'd have had time to sort things out. Testing a new plane was one thing. Before he went up, he knew everything there was to know and had figured the odds right down to the smallest decimal. This time he was flying blind.

Odds? He hadn't even known there were any.

Before supper, Keegan, Brace and Sharon had talked shop while Maudie fed the baby and Frances set out the food. Things had gone surprisingly well. They could have been deuced awkward, considering the circumstances. Keegan seemed amused at Sharon's aggressiveness. She knew her business and didn't mind airing her ideas. Listening to her, watching her small square hands chop the air as she made a point, Brace thought about the decision that was still to be made. Any project Sharon Bing was involved in would pay off, one way or another. The woman had a steel-trap mind. He could do worse than to team up with Bing Aero.

His gaze strayed to Frances, and he caught a look on her face that touched a resonating chord. Something was bothering her—the shadows were back in her eyes—but she felt it, too. The warmth. The harmony. The palpable bond between Keegan, his Maudie and their son.

Keegan brought the boy back with him and was bouncing him on his knee while Sharon's strident voice hammered home a point about aerodynamic design versus tensile strength. The Chief's tiny, star-shaped hands explored his father's nose, and Brace caught Fancy's eyes with a slow, kindling smile.

Peace. It wasn't always the result of treaties or conferences or peace-keeping troops. Things could be pretty simple once a man learned to stop looking for answers to every question and made a private treaty with life.

It was barely ten when Keegan stifled a yawn. Brace, remembering the length of their day, caught Frances's eye again and nodded to the door. Sharon, now launched on a monologue about a new system of inventory control she'd designed—single-handed, if you believed her—and how much it had saved the company over a three-year period, leaned forward in her chair, eyes glittering like faceted aquamarines.

"Time to cut out," he said, interrupting. "I'll see you two home."

Sharon looked up at him blankly. "I was just telling Rich about—"

"It can wait. They've had a long day." He grinned when Keegan could no longer hold back his yawn.

"Well, pardon me!" Sharon snapped. Rising, she smoothed her gray gabardine suit over her hips. "Sorry if I bored you."

Brace cut off Keegan's perfunctory denial. "Come on—moon's up now, we won't even need a flashlight." Frances, who'd been loading her clean empty dishes in her basket, glanced over her shoulder and smiled as they both recalled her tiny pink purse light.

But then, even as he watched, the laughter faded from her eyes, leaving them a little sad, a little wary. He swore silently, suspecting part of it, at least, was his fault.

The wind had dropped off to nothing, the temperature had risen, and a three-quarter moon shone brightly through the branches of live oaks and loblolly pines. Near the edge of the softly lapping water, the ghost of a long-dead cedar stood like a silvery sentinel against the night.

This has to be the most peaceful place in the universe, Frances thought. As impossible as it would have seemed only a few weeks ago, she would be sorry to leave when the time came.

Green, thought Brace. Funny—he'd never associated fragrance with color before, but hers was definitely green, with a hint of spice. Not heavy—barely there, but unmistakably hers.

Sharon wore one of the designer fragrances that came on too strong, too sweet and too cloying. It had always seemed an odd choice for a woman who could hold her own in a room full of engineers and financial experts. But then, what did he know about women? Not as much as he'd thought—that much was growing clearer by the minute.

"God, this place gives me the creeps!" Sharon muttered. "Why would anyone choose to live here of their own free will?"

They reached the cottage, and Brace, who'd been carrying Frances's basket, set it on the railing. Not bothering to hide his impatience, he said, "Be ready by nine tomorrow. I'll run you across and make arrangements to get you to Norfolk." He turned to Frances, and they waited for the other woman to leave. When she didn't, he said, "Sharon, maybe you'd better pack now in case you oversleep."

The moment they were alone together, Brace reached for Frances. Her arms came up around his neck as if they'd been forceably restrained all night long, and he held her tightly against his hard, hungry body. "How did everything get so screwed up?" he whispered, and then made it impossible for her to reply.

A long time later when he lifted his head, he continued to sift his fingers through her hair, savoring the sensuous feel of its silken weight. "I'm thinking a lot of stuff right now—stuff I don't know how to say without sounding like a fool. Just in case you were wondering." His eyes crinkled down at her, and he uttered a husky, embarrassed sort of laugh. "Stuff about your eyes and your skin and your hair—about the difference between pretty and beautiful. I never even knew there was a difference before, isn't that crazy?"

Frances hadn't the least notion of what he was talking about, she only knew she was back where she belonged. Against all reason she was back in his arms, and she wasn't about to rock the boat by asking foolish questions.

"Remember when I said I wasn't offering you anything?"

She nodded. "And I told you I wasn't asking you for anything. And I meant it."

"Yeah, well—the thing is, maybe I—"

The door opened at his back, and Sharon stepped outside. "Brace, I think I left my good pen over at the Keegans'. I had it out diagramming the fuel line on the R-40, remember? I must have— "

"Judas priest, Sharon, go to bed!"

"You don't have to bite my head off. It happens to be my favorite pen. I paid over two hundred dollars for it, and—"

"I'll bring it over in the morning, all right? Now, for cripe's sake, will you please go to bed?"

She moved a step closer and slipped her arm through his. "Is that an offer, darling?" she purred, and he swore again.

"Look, Fancy, I'll see you when I get back, all right? We'll pick up where we left off."

"Fancy, hmm?" The two women watched the tall male figure stalk off in the moonlight, and then Sharon began to laugh. "Fancy. I like it. Pity there's nothing you can do with my name. Share never did appeal." The look in her pale blue-green eyes lent the words meaning that followed Frances into a long, sleepless night.

Don't make the same mistake again, she told herself as she lay in her bed, trying in vain to recapture the warmth she'd felt so recently.

The trouble was, the mistake had already been made. Her immune system, battered from past experience, had been no match at all for a man like Brace Ridgeway.

Ten

Frances waited. An hour to get there, an hour back—it shouldn't take all that long, even if he'd had to drive her to the airstrip and arrange a charter. While she waited, she turned out the second bedroom and gave it a good airing. It reeked of her least favorite perfume.

She shampooed her hair, applied a cucumber-and-oatmeal mask to her face and buffed her fingernails until they shone.

And then she baked a perfectly sinful double-chocolate cake using cherry preserves in the filling. Somehow the occasion seemed to call for refined sugar, refined flour, fat-and-caffeine-laden chocolate, artificial coloring and a bundle of preservatives and stabilizers. Her body craved it!

She finished frosting the cake just before dark, admired it for a few minutes, cried for a few more and then took it to Rich and Maudie. The weather had turned again, the temperature was plummeting, and the clouds had moved in just before sunset. It seemed somehow appropriate.

"Are you sure you want to give it all away?" Maudie asked. Her face was flushed, her top three buttons undone, and there was a suspicious-looking red area on the side of her throat, as though someone who hadn't shaved since morning had been nuzzling her there.

Frances felt the tears threaten again. For nearly forty years, she'd hardly shed more than a dozen tears, but lately she was making up for lost time.

"Take it—please," she begged. "If you don't, I'll just eat it all."

"Brace should be back in a couple of days. I'm pretty sure it'll keep that long if you turn a dishpan down over it." Even the best equipped cottage seldom ran to cake domes.

"So let him eat bread." Frances shrugged, managed a little half smile, and hurried back to Blackbeard's Hole.

With the manuscript in the mail—she'd been warned by a romance writer she knew not to look for any response for at least a month—Frances settled down with a new batch of classified ads to respond to all the possibles and a few not-so-possibles. The job market was pathetic. Anyone with a halfway decent job had the good sense to hang on to it. She should have thought twice about turning in her resignation and giving away her house.

And to think she'd once claimed to be the sensible member of the clan. No wonder she'd gotten herself into such a mess—she had the brains of a doorknob!

By bedtime she had circled seven ads in three newspapers and written responses to four of them, updating her résumés to include her new publishing credit. During breakfast the following morning, she wrote the last three letters and got them ready to mail. That made seventeen jobs she'd applied for in five cities and seven counties. Of the seventeen, she was overqualified for eleven and underqualified for two—not very encouraging. Her résumé, with its handwritten addenda, wasn't the neatest thing in the world, but at least her credentials were respectable.

She had planned to run over to the post office, but one look at the choppy water changed her mind. Instead, she dropped the letters off at the Hunt for Rich to mail the next time he made a supply run.

And then she walked. With a cold wind howling in from the northwest and the spray flying halfway up the beach, she decided it was the perfect time to explore the island. So what if her gaze happened to linger longest on the Hatteras side, where the marina could barely be seen in the distance? It was only because there was nothing else to see. Water, water, everywhere and not—

"Oh, for pity's sake," she muttered angrily.

Thawing out in a tub of hot water some half an hour later, Frances told herself that if experience was such a great teacher, she must have flunked the course. He hadn't promised her anything. In fact, he'd made a point of *not* promising her anything—which was a darned sight better, she supposed, than promising her the moon and then reneging. Still, you'd think she'd know better than to stick her hand into the fire again.

Actually she should be grateful. If he hadn't had the decency to warn her, she'd probably be picking out a new trousseau and wondering whether to be married in a dressy dress or a tailored suit. "Face it—after three strikes, even a Little League tyro would know she was out."

Frances didn't want to face it. "It's only sex, for goodness sake! They teach it in grade school these days!"

Only sex? Sure, and earthquakes were only earthquakes, and rainbows were only rainbows. And Mount Pinatubo was only...

With a sound somewhere between a sob and a chuckle, she slithered down in the bathtub until the water closed over her head.

Only sex. You'd think neither of them had ever done it before, the way it had turned out that first time. A lot of fumbling, a lot of heavy breathing, and then— whamo! And the crazy thing was, it hadn't mattered. Being left hanging was nothing new, but this time, she hadn't been left with that half empty, half angry feeling. It had been enough that they were together at all. That he hadn't left her right away to go to his own bed. That he had held her and talked to her and loved her again, loved her so completely that even her toenails had sizzled.

And then loved her yet again.

She sat up in the tub, her hair plastered over her eyes, and told herself that regardless of what else he was—or wasn't—no man had ever been so generous. No man had ever taken the time to understand and cater to her needs. Frances knew she should be grateful that he had given her as much of himself as he had, and she tried to be. Honestly she did. But she was greedy. She wanted more. She wanted *all* of him, not just his sexuality.

And not just for a single night.

If one needed to cry, then the bath was as good a place as any to do it. Ever practical, Frances cried until she couldn't breathe through her nose, and then she pulled off several yards of tissue and blew, wiped her eyes and let the lukewarm bathwater gurgle down the drain. She felt limp and cold and tired and a little bit hungry, but at least she'd worked him out of her system.

Tomorrow would be time enough to clean the cottage and pack her bags. The next day she would move over to Hatteras and make arrangements with the Keegans to redirect her mail in care of general delivery until she could relocate. It was pretty much what she'd planned to do all along. Finish her book, get it off and then start job and apartment hunting. Nothing had really changed.

Brace took time to go shopping after his final meeting. He bought slacks and a blazer, a couple of suits that would probably gather moss in his closet, and all the trimmings. He bought a bottle of cologne, a bottle of champagne and a box of imported chocolates.

He bought a ring. Nothing really showy, but special. He picked out the stones, and over the jeweler's disapproval of his choices, had them set in white gold. *Nobody,* the man said, put amethysts and sapphires together. It just wasn't done!

Brace did it. Amethysts to match her eyes, sapphires to match her character and diamonds because they looked good with the darker stones.

He told himself he was jumping the gun and then went ahead and jumped it. He thought about a lot of things he'd never thought about before—things like tenderness, honesty and steadfastness. Things like a woman's laughter, a woman's sadness, a woman's warmth and friendship.

For the first time since—well, hell! For the first time since forever!—Brace thought of what it would be like to share the rest of his life, the good times and the not so good times, with a woman like Fancy Smith. Logic told him he was coming in way too high, way too fast, but instinct told him he could make it if he held steady on his present heading.

For a man who'd been dumped, patched up and put out to pasture not all that long ago, he felt good. He felt better than good, he felt *righteous!*

By the time he crossed the state line into North Carolina, he was singing along with a country music station, and Brace hadn't sung a note since he'd been thrown out of a Lightfoot concert back in the seventies for trying to climb up on stage and sing harmony with the star.

"Are you serious?" Frances cried into the receiver. Maudie had dropped by to report on the demolition and appreciation of the cake just as a call from her editor came through. "But I just overnighted it to you—you haven't even had time to read it yet!"

And then, with Maudie unabashedly eavesdropping, she said again, "Are you serious? Of course I can do it! You really like my style enough to—"

"To what?" Maudie whispered loudly.

"No, I don't have an agent, but—"

"A movie deal?" Maudie's green eyes rounded as she perched on the arm of the chair and tried to hear both ends of the conversation. When Frances hung up a few minutes later, Maudie shouted, "What! What!

You're going to be a movie star, is that it? They want you to get an agent and go out to Hollywood and—''

"They want to know how fast I can do another cookbook," Frances said in a dazed tone. "Before they've even read the whole manuscript for my first one, they've decided to do a series. *Fancy's Fat-Free*, followed by *Fancy's Frugal* and— Oh, all sorts of possibilities!"

"Do they all have to start with an *F*? That kind of limits your choices, doesn't it? Fruit? Fowl? Fish? Frogs?"

Flopping back on the hard daybed, Frances tried to remember every word of the conversation. She felt like a cola that had been shaken hard and then opened. Fizzing out all over the place. "She liked my style. They have this idea about a cover treatment—I've forgotten what she said about it, or maybe she didn't say. Anyway, she said I need to find an agent, and they want a three-book contract, and how soon can I get started on the next one?"

"So where's your typewriter, woman?"

"Packed, and it's not a typewriter, it's a—"

"So what about you and Brace?"

Suddenly, the fizz went out of the cola. If anything could have brought her back down again, it was that.

After Maudie left to go feed the Chief—he was well into solid foods and partial to chair rungs at the moment—she told herself that the news couldn't have come at a better time. She desperately needed the money, but she needed the distraction even more.

Brace. If she'd thought the mere shedding of a gallon or so of tears would wash him out of her system, she couldn't have been more wrong.

Frances had known Paul Capro for a year and a half before they'd almost become engaged. She'd known Adam eight months before they'd become lovers, and Kenneth—goodness, she'd known Ken for at least four years before they'd married, only to find out she hadn't really known him at all.

So why was it that a man she had known only a few weeks—a man who had done his best to scare her away—a man who had started out disliking her as much as she had disliked him—could slip in under her guard when she wasn't looking and wind up stealing her heart?

Paul and Adam were only dim faces from the past. Like faded photographs from an old album. Looking back, she couldn't even remember why she'd been attracted to them.

And Ken. Well, she knew why she'd been drawn to him, of course. He'd been so considerate of his parents, and she'd thought that any man who took the time to visit his mother several times a week and call her once a day would make a kind and considerate husband.

And, too, he'd been handsome in a bland, blond sort of way.

So why Brace? He wasn't always kind—though he could be. He wasn't always considerate. Look how he'd climbed in and out of her bed and then walked off without so much as a thank-you-ma'am when another woman came along. He certainly wasn't handsome. At least, not in any conventional way.

Unfortunately he also wasn't a man a woman could ever forget. There was no well-groomed facade to disguise his basic nature. He was real all the way through.

Flaws and all, he was the kind of man that no woman, having once loved him, could ever forget.

If she'd had a functioning brain, she would have cut and run the first time he'd tried to scare her off. Unfortunately, her survival skills had been too rusty to recognize the true nature of the threat.

Thank God and a discerning editor for a project that would engage all her energies for the foreseeable future. Wherever she decided to settle down—and it really didn't matter as long as it was cheap and there was a phone, a post office, a fax and a decent supermarket—she'd be too busy to think about anything but her new contract.

And if she cried a few more tears in the night, what difference would it make? It would clear her sinuses, if nothing else.

After a sketchy supper, she pored over the classified section again, this time trying to get a feel for the cost of living in various places, until her eyelids began to droop. A few more minutes and she was asleep at the table amidst a scattering of rumpled newspapers and a half-eaten sandwich.

It was the sound of a mosquito that brought her half-awake again.

A mosquito? In February?

An outboard.

In the middle of the night?

Yawning, she stood up, stretched and glanced at the clock. A quarter of ten. Time for bed. Any major decisions would have to wait until morning. She was crawling into bed, teeth brushed, face scrubbed and moisturized, and her hair wild from fifty-seven strokes with a boar bristle brush when she heard someone

banging on her front door. Even before she flipped the
night latch, she knew who was on the other side, the
same way she had known there were monsters under
her bed when she was five. She'd simply *known* it, that
was all.

"Brace, what are you... *Brace?*"

She stared at the well-dressed stranger on her doorstep. His hair had been trimmed—not too short, not
too long. He was wearing a pair of dark gray flannels
with a navy blazer and an open necked shirt. With his
perfect nose and his offset cheekbones and his crooked
grin, he looked good enough to eat—all zillion and a
half calories of him.

So much for survival skills. "Oh, for goodness sake,
you might as well come inside," she muttered ungra-
ciously, tugging her flannel bathrobe tighter around her
old Save the Whales nightshirt. One of these days she
was going to buy herself a red satin nightgown. Bias
cut. With red lace straps!

"I didn't wake you, did I?" He hesitated a second
and followed her inside.

"It doesn't matter. I wasn't really asleep." Back to
square one. He was embarrassed, and so was she. At
least he was no longer trying to run her off. He'd already taken care of that.

"I—uh, hey, maybe I'd better wait until tomorrow?" he ventured. The mask was back in place. She
only hoped hers was, too.

"Whatever you've come to say, Brace, you might as
well say it now." Deliberately, she continued to stand,
making it impossible for him to sit down. She switched
on the overhead light and saw his eyes narrow against
the glare. If he thought he could just drop in any time
he took a notion to and hop back into her bed, he'd

better think again. Just because she'd made a mistake once didn't mean she had to go on repeating it.

"What's with the Apartment to Rent?"

He'd picked up one of the newspapers and was frowning at it while she tried to ignore the way his blazer fit his wide shoulders and skimmed the lean, hard contours of his torso. "The ads? I'll be leaving here in a day or so. I thought I might check out a few possibilities."

"Leave here! Why?"

And when she only stared, he said, "But you can't! Not yet. What's your hurry, anyway?"

He looked so genuinely shaken, she blurted the first thing that came to mind. "Brace, have you had anything to eat?"

Oh, for goodness sake, she was going to have stop trying to feed every stray that wandered in off the streets! "Forget I said that," she muttered.

"You're taking back your invitation?"

Old habits died hard. She opened the bread box and pulled out a loaf of raisin pumpernickle. "I suppose I could make you a sandwich if you're hungry. You'll probably wake Maudie and the baby if you go rummaging around in her kitchen."

"I'm not hungry—not for food."

Something in the resonance of his voice raised every nerve ending in her body. Frances knew for a fact that the sky was clear. It was littered with stars, yet the air felt the same way it had when that unseasonal thunderstorm had raced through nearly a week before.

She took a step back. "I think you'd better go."

"No way. I'm not leaving now."

"Brace, I don't want—"

"But I do, Fancy. I do want."

Anger, tinged with fear and colored with excitement, swept over her. Feeling her nipples harden, she crossed her arms over her breasts. "You're old enough to know you don't always get what you want. If you're hungry, I'll feed you. If you have something to say, I'll listen, but that's it. I have a big day coming up, and I'd just as soon get a good night's sleep first."

"You won't sleep and you know it. No more than I will." The mask had slipped. Somewhere deep in the clear gray depths of his eyes, a gleam was born, a gleam that made her feel distinctly wary.

"Dammit, Brace, why couldn't you have had the common decency to stay away until I was safely gone?"

"Y'know, somehow I never took you for a coward. I figured you for a lot of things. Independent. Reckless. Stubborn. But I never figured you for a coward. What are you so scared of, Fancy?"

"Don't call me that!" The name on his tongue conjured up images that had nothing at all to do with cooking. Fancy's Feckless Foibles came instantly to mind.

Brace removed his coat and tossed it at a chair, where it slid to the floor. He ignored it. Frances stepped back, not trusting the hungry gleam in his eyes. She shivered.

"Cold?" he growled suggestively, lifting his split-level eyebrow.

"No, I'm not cold, I'm hot as a firecracker!" She meant hot as in angry, but naturally, he took it another way. Grinning, he began to stalk her. Around the sofa, around the big chair—behind the table. He had the advantage. She couldn't see where she was going. When she backed into the utility room door and tried to slide away, two strong arms came up to block her escape.

Hands on the doorframe, Brace moved in for the kill. "Don't look so scared, precious, I'm not going to force you."

"No," she said breathlessly. "I knew that. It's— umm, it's been nice knowing you, and I wish you luck with your new job with the Bings, and will you please latch the door on your way out?"

His smile was purely predatory. It made the skin on her nape tingle. "It's been nice knowing you, too, Fancy. I wish us both luck with the future, but I never bank solely on luck. The time comes when a man has to make his own luck."

"Yes, well...whatever." She could barely speak above a whisper. There was a hard, aching lump in her chest that was making it impossible to breathe.

"Whatever, Fancy?" His voice caressed her like a mink glove. "You mean that?"

"It's a figure of speech, for goodness sake! Brace, you're not making sense, I think you'd better leave. I—"

"You what, Fancy? You mean you really don't know why I'm here? But you knew I'd be back, didn't you?"

Wordlessly she shook her head, unable to look away.

"You knew we weren't finished."

"But Sharon—"

"Forget Sharon. She's nothing to do with us."

"Us?" she whispered faintly. Her stomach growled. She saw the corner of his mouth quirk in that funny way he had, and she could have died. "Oh, damn, damn, damn," she muttered. "This isn't the way it was supposed to happen."

He didn't ask what—he didn't have to. Instead, he asked how. And she told him. "I was supposed to be dressed in something slinky and expensive, and you were supposed to fall on your knees and—"

"Allow me a cushion, and I might manage one knee."

"Oh, hush up! It was just a silly daydream, and I'm too old to daydream, and besides, I've never been any good at it."

"Haven't you?" he asked, and she could have sworn it was tenderness that made his voice sound like a warm fog. "Funny... I've just discovered a talent for day-dreaming. And night dreaming. And do you know what I dream about, Fancy lady?"

"Airplanes and hot sauce and— Brace, do you have to do that?"

He was openly grinning now, his face close and coming closer. "Yeah, I think I do." And closer... "And this," he whispered just as his mouth closed over hers, moist, firm, warmly demanding.

His hands were on her shoulders, circling, smooth-ing, his thumbs brushing the sensitive hollows where her neck joined her shoulders. As she felt his surging need, her last rational thought fled and she clung to him, answering need with need.

"Brace, this isn't any good," she gasped when she could speak again. She had her future all tidy and ac-counted for, and he'd had to come along and remind her all over again of what she'd be missing. It wasn't fair!

"Shh, it's good," he soothed, and then he was lead-ing her into the bedroom, and she could no more resist him than molasses could run uphill.

This time he made love to her slowly, leading her to the edge of madness again and again. Making her plead. "We have all night, sweetheart. There's no hurry."

Demented, she fought him for control, and he let her win and then laughed at her. But when she rolled him onto his back and moved over him, his laughter ceased. He caught his breath and closed his eyes, and she felt a sense of power unlike anything she had ever felt before.

He guided her. And when she was frantic, and lost control of the rhythm, he rolled them onto their sides, and with a skillful interweaving of limbs, the dance resumed. This time he led and she followed. His hands were on her hips, his teeth against her throat as he arched his back and drove them both home. And when it was over, he gathered her tightly against him, hearts pounding in tandem, sweat mingling, laughter and sobs breaking the sudden silence.

A long time later he tilted her face to his, and she met his gaze—love, a little sadness and a lot of joy all there to see. "This is only a small part of it," he whispered. "Now do you understand what I'm trying to say?"

Numbly she shook her head. She understood only that she would never, ever get over loving this man. If she never saw him again, a hundred years from now she would still remember the way he looked when he was angry, the way he looked when he was amused, the way he looked when he forgot and dropped his guard. She would never forget the way he looked when he was teasing her about her recipes, playing with the baby, talking flying with Rich Keegan.

Or the way he looked when he had just made love to her.

"Fancy? I'm not getting much feedback here. A guy feels sort of out on a limb at a time like this."

"No more than a woman does. Brace, I...I..." The words were on the tip of her tongue, aching to be spoken, but she knew better. She would bite her tongue off before she'd tell him and watch the mask slip back in place again.

Her eyes widened suddenly. "At a time like what?"

"Got your attention, did I?" He grinned. "At a time when he's trying to tell his woman how much he loves her without sounding like a third-rate actor reading a fourth-rate script."

Frances felt as if she were in a vacuum—as if all the air had suddenly been sucked from the room. "He could just—just say it, couldn't he?"

"Yeah, I reckon he could. It's not like he hasn't practiced his lines, only they sound sort of...pretentious."

"Bra-a-ace, say it!"

"Yeah, well...here goes." He cleared his throat, and Frances felt her eyes brim over, felt her heart swell until it nearly burst.

He cleared his throat again, and when she couldn't stand it another second, she blurted, "Don't you even know how much I love you? I thought I'd *die* trying to keep from telling you!" She was laughing and crying as a crazy sort of joyousness began to fill her whole being.

Gathering her into his arms again, he buried his face in the cool silk of her hair and whispered hoarsely, "Me, too. God, sweetheart, I never even knew what hit me until it was almost too late, but I finally figured it out. *Me, too!*"

It wasn't particularly romantic, but from a man with a perfect nose and a split-level eyebrow—a man who doused his dinner with hot sauce and fell asleep over old World War II training films, it was more than enough. She'd had the moonlight and roses, and it hadn't lasted. She'd had all the sweet, glib, lying words. This time she would gladly settle for an honest, heartfelt "Me, too!"

Long after Frances had fallen asleep in his arms, Brace lay awake, smiling into the darkness. He loved her so damned much it flat-out knocked him off his pins. One of these days he might even be able to tell her without sounding like a fool.

Until then, he'd just have to prove it to her. If it took two lifetimes, he'd make certain she knew it—make sure she never forgot it. Lessons learned late in life were the sweetest lessons of all, he mused. And the most enduring.

*   *   *   *   *

COMING NEXT MONTH

#895 AN OBSOLETE MAN—Lass Small

December's *Man of the Month*, rugged Clinton Terrell, had only
sexy Wallis Witherspoon on his mind. So he trapped her on a ranch,
determined to make this irresistible intellectual *his!*

#896 THE HEADSTRONG BRIDE—Joan Johnston

Children of Hawk's Way

When rancher Sam Longstreet hoodwinked curvaceous Callen Whitelaw
into marrying him, he had only wanted revenge. But it didn't take long
before he was falling for his headstrong bride!

#897 HOMETOWN WEDDING—Pamela Macaluso

Just Married!

Callie Harrison vowed to marry bad boy Rorke O'Neil years ago, but
she bailed out before the wedding. Now Rorke was back with a secret—
one Callie might not be able to forgive....

#898 MURDOCK'S FAMILY—Paula Detmer Riggs

When divorced Navy SEAL Cairn Murdock's family was threatened, he
raced to their sides. Nothing, not even the burning secret he held, would
prevent him from keeping the woman he'd never stopped loving safe....

#899 DARK INTENTIONS—Carole Buck

Sweet Julia Kendricks decided to help Royce Williams adjust to life in
darkness after he lost his eyesight. But soon *he* was helping *her* see his
true intentions....

#900 SEDUCED—Metsy Hingle

Michael Grayson didn't need love, but he *did* need a wife, in order to
keep custody of his niece. So he seduced sophisticated Amanda Bennett,
never expecting to fall for the fiery woman....

JINGLE BELLS, WEDDING BELLS:
Silhouette's Christmas Collection for 1994

Christmas Wish List

*To beat the crowds at the malls and get the perfect present for *everyone,* even that snoopy Mrs. Smith next door!

*To get through the holiday parties without running my panty hose.

*To bake cookies, decorate the house and serve the perfect Christmas dinner—just like the women in all those magazines.

*To sit down, curl up and read my Silhouette Christmas stories!

Join *New York Times* bestselling author Nora Roberts, along with popular writers Barbara Boswell, Myrna Temte and Elizabeth August, as we celebrate the joys of Christmas—and the magic of marriage—with

JINGLE BELLS, WEDDING BELLS

Silhouette's Christmas Collection for 1994.

 Silhouette®

JBWB

CHILDREN OF

series continues with
THE HEADSTRONG BRIDE
by Joan Johnston

Rancher Sam Longstreet knew Garth Whitelaw was responsible for his family's troubles. And he set out to even the score. Sam planned to sweep young Callie Whitelaw off her feet and marry her. But he hadn't bargained on *loving* his headstrong bride!

Look for *The Headstrong Bride,* book two of the CHILDREN OF HAWK'S WAY miniseries, coming your

**Another wonderful year of romance
concludes with**

Christmas
Memories

Share in the magic and memories of romance
during the holiday season with this collection of two
full-length contemporary Christmas stories,
by two bestselling authors

**Diana Palmer
Marilyn Pappano**

Available in December at your favorite retail outlet.

Only from **Silhouette®**

TM

where passion lives.

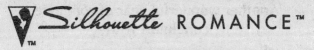

Silhouette ROMANCE™

'Tis the season for romantic bliss.
It all begins with just one kiss—

UNDER THE MISTLETOE

Celebrate the joy of the season and the thrill of romance with this special collection:

Available in December, from Silhouette Romance.

SRXMAS

"HOORAY FOR HOLLYWOOD" SWEEPSTAKES

HERE'S HOW THE SWEEPSTAKES WORKS

OFFICIAL RULES — NO PURCHASE NECESSARY

To enter, complete an Official Entry Form or hand print on a 3" x 5" card the words "HOORAY FOR HOLLYWOOD", your name and address and mail your entry in the pre-addressed envelope (if provided) or to: "Hooray for Hollywood" Sweepstakes, P.O. Box 9076, Buffalo, NY 14269-9076 or "Hooray for Hollywood" Sweepstakes, P.O. Box 637, Fort Erie, Ontario L2A 5X3. Entries must be sent via First Class Mail and be received no later than 12/31/94. No liability is assumed for lost, late or misdirected mail.

Winners will be selected in random drawings to be conducted no later than January 31, 1995 from all eligible entries received.

Grand Prize: A 7-day/6-night trip for 2 to Los Angeles, CA including round trip air transportation from commercial airport nearest winner's residence, accommodations at the Regent Beverly Wilshire Hotel, free rental car, and $1,000 spending money. (Approximate prize value which will vary dependent upon winner's residence: $5,400.00 U.S.); 500 Second Prizes: A pair of "Hollywood Star" sunglasses (prize value: $9.95 U.S. each). Winner selection is under the supervision of D.L. Blair, Inc., an independent judging organization, whose decisions are final. Grand Prize travelers must sign and return a release of liability prior to traveling. Trip must be taken by 2/1/96 and is subject to airline schedules and accommodations availability.

Sweepstakes offer is open to residents of the U.S. (except Puerto Rico) and Canada who are 18 years of age or older, except employees and immediate family members of Harlequin Enterprises, Ltd., its affiliates, subsidiaries, and all agencies, entities or persons connected with the use, marketing or conduct of this sweepstakes. All federal, state, provincial, municipal and local laws apply. Offer void wherever prohibited by law. Taxes and/or duties are the sole responsibility of the winners. Any litigation within the province of Quebec respecting the conduct and awarding of prizes may be submitted to the Regie des loteries et courses du Quebec. All prizes will be awarded; winners will be notified by mail. No substitution of prizes are permitted. Odds of winning are dependent upon the number of eligible entries received.

Potential grand prize winner must sign and return an Affidavit of Eligibility within 30 days of notification. In the event of non-compliance within this time period, prize may be awarded to an alternate winner. Prize notification returned as undeliverable may result in the awarding of prize to an alternate winner. By acceptance of their prize, winners consent to use of their names, photographs, or likenesses for purpose of advertising, trade and promotion on behalf of Harlequin Enterprises, Ltd., without further compensation unless prohibited by law. A Canadian winner must correctly answer an arithmetical skill-testing question in order to be awarded the prize.

For a list of winners (available after 2/28/95), send a separate stamped, self-addressed envelope to: Hooray for Hollywood Sweepstakes 3252 Winners, P.O. Box 4200, Blair, NE 68009.

CBSRLS

OFFICIAL ENTRY COUPON

"Hooray for Hollywood"
SWEEPSTAKES!

Yes, I'd love to win the Grand Prize — a vacation in Hollywood —
or one of 500 pairs of "sunglasses of the stars"! Please enter me
in the sweepstakes!

This entry must be received by December 31, 1994.
Winners will be notified by January 31, 1995.

Name _____

Address _____ Apt. _____

City _____

State/Prov. _____ Zip/Postal Code _____

Daytime phone number _____
(area code)

Account # _____

Return entries with invoice in envelope provided. Each book
in this shipment has two entry coupons — and the more
coupons you enter, the better your chances of winning!

DIRCBS